Something I Need to Tell You

William Thirsk-Gaskill

Stairwell Books
///

Published by Stairwell Books
70 Barbara Drive
Norwalk
CT 06851 USA

161 Lowther Street
York, YO31 7LZ

www.stairwellbooks.co.uk
@stairwellbooks

ISBN: 978-1-939269-64-5

Printed and bound in the UK by Imprint Digital
Layout design: Alan Gillott
Cover Image: 'Wilson'

Acknowledgements

'How to be an Alcoholic' published in *Best British Short Stories 2018,* Salt Publications, Nicholas Royle editor;

'Slow Dance With a Skeleton' won 2nd place out of over 1000 entries in the *Grist* 2012 short fiction competition;

'Can We Have You All Sitting Down, Please?' published in *Crying Just Like Anybody*, Fiction Desk, 2012

Table of Contents

The Girl from V17

My name is Orion. I don't know how old I am. I have just woken up. This is my favourite time of day. I am lying on my side in bed, looking at my mother, who is still asleep. Our house is a dustbin. It is made of green plastic and we turned it on its side before we started to live in it. I can see my mother in the morning sunlight because it is June, and so we have the door propped open at the moment. We close the door when it rains. I like it better when we can have the door open. The birds are still singing, but they have quietened down a bit. The sky is clear. It is going to be a hot day. I am getting up now, quietly, so as not to wake my mother. She had a hard day, yesterday.

We have two tunnels to get out of the place where we live, which is in a gulley between two mounds in a part of The Village called The Nature Sanctuary. We are surrounded by gorse and reeds and elder and sycamore saplings and a lot of nettles, and so our house is completely hidden. We make the tunnels by weaving twigs together or cutting back the new growth so that the way stays clear, and we can get in and out without rustling any branches. Like most of the forest, the ground is covered with old, fallen leaves which are flat and springy for most of the year and keep your footsteps nearly silent.

I walk through the west tunnel as far as the place where you have to crawl, and then I go the last part of the way on my hands and knees. I stand up behind a big butterfly-bush, and then I listen carefully to hear if anybody is coming. I am listening for the whirr of a laundry-cart, or the sound of a tractor or car engine, or footsteps, or voices. All I can hear is birdsong. I slip out onto the path. My mother has a word for how I am supposed to do this: *nonchalantly*. That means I have to do it without letting anybody know that I am a Human and not a Guest. Guests look exactly like Humans, except for their clothes, and sometimes you see them inside cars or vans, and they can go in all the places where the Guests are allowed, without being cast out. To stay alive, my mother and I have to avoid being cast out. That means that I must not let anybody know I am a Human, and I must learn the Litany.

1

I will go back to the Litany after I have been for a walk and found some breakfast. The next bit should be interesting: it explains how many Humans there are, and how big the world is, and how our Tribe (that is me and my mother) ended up where we are.

Most of the Litany is dead boring. I like to read it by torchlight, last thing at night. I have a torch and a battery-charger. We get our electricity from a thing that my mother connects to a lamp-post on the path to the Nature Sanctuary.

*

For breakfast, I have had two slices of Meat Feast pizza with the topping still on, a few crusts, a jam doughnut, some very ripe bananas, and a pear which had almost turned to mush but was still all right to eat. I got them from a bin near Cabin X89. I quite often look through the bins of the "X" Cabins: they tend to have more stuff in them. It is amazing what some of the Guests throw away. My mother says that their wastefulness is evidence of their Sin.

When I had eaten all that, I was really thirsty, and so I went to the stream that we call The Dribble, and had a drink, and filled my water-bottle.

I had a walk round the Driving Range, and the Sports Arena, and by the side of the Boating Lake and the Village Green, which was my usual route. It was still early and not many of the Guests were about. I was looking for Cabin V17. I knew that Cabin V17 was where Lorna was staying. I wanted to see Lorna again. My mother keeps telling me that Lorna is a Guest, but I don't believe her. I am sure that Lorna is Human. She has just got to be Human.

Lorna is the only person I have spoken to, apart from myself, and my mother, and one of the Keepers who spoke to me a few weeks ago, in as long as I can remember. The conversation with the Keeper really shook me up, but my mother was pleased with me.

'Are you lost?' he asked me. I didn't know whether he thought I was a Guest, or if he knew I was Human. If he knew I was Human, his question would have meant, 'Do you know you have lost the Struggle?' My heart was racing, and I was sweating and shaking, and my teeth were chattering, but I forced myself to answer – nonchalantly.

'I'm fine: I'm just looking for the next point in the Number Quest.' I held up a sheet of paper I had just taken out of my trouser pocket. The Keeper smiled. I had deliberately said that, because I knew that the

Keepers are not allowed to help Guests who are taking part in the Number Quest. He left me alone.

The conversation with Lorna made me just as nervous, but in a different way.

I was sweeping some peanuts off a bird table into a paper cup, and looking round to see if anybody could see me. It was later than I usually look for food, and some of the Guests were getting up and starting to move around. I saw her through a window in Cabin V17. She was getting dressed. She is about as tall as me, and she has brown skin and brown eyes and long, black, curly hair. I hid. I waited for her to come out. I was worried that her mother and a man and some other children would come out as well. They did. I stayed hidden. They went out somewhere. I listened to what they were saying, but I could not work out where they were going. I couldn't really understand what they were talking about. I waited. They were gone for hours. My mother came. She was wearing the clothes that she uses to disguise herself as a Guest. She asked me what I was doing. I knew I had to tell her a lie.

'I thought I saw a slow-worm,' I said, pointing to a clump of bushes. 'I was waiting for it to come out again.' My mother likes it when I do things that mean waiting and watching the same spot for hours and hours, even if it means that in the end nothing happens. She went away again, which was exactly what I wanted her to do. I carried on waiting.

Lorna and her family came back, and Lorna walked out of the back of the Cabin, towards the lake. She was by herself. I pretended to be walking by the shore of the lake, past the back of her Cabin. I was trying to think of something to say to her, when she spoke to me.

'Hi. Where ya goin'?' Her voice sounded funny, almost as if she was singing instead of talking. My mother does not allow singing. She says it makes too much noise and might lead to us being found and cast out.

'Walking round the lake,' I replied. I was very glad I had not clammed-up.

'Can I come, too?'

'Of course you can.'

Lorna and I started talking to each other as we walked.

'What's your name?'

'Orion.'

'That's a cool name. I'm Lorna.'

'Lorna.'

'That's right. Where do you come from?'

'Round here.'

'Oh. Where do you go to school?'

'Round here.'

'So you have come on holiday to Lincoln Green Adventure Village, even though you live round here?'

'Er. Yes.'

'That's weird. But nice. It is weird in a nice way, not a weird weird way. You should start a website: www.notinaweirdweirdway.co.uk'.

'Start a website? What, you mean, like a spider does?' She laughed. I can't stop thinking about that moment. I don't know why she laughed, but I think I made her happy.

*

Here I am at Cabin V17, and I have the best view into the Cabin because I can hide behind a tree but still see in through the big window. I can see Lorna and the Guests that she came with. I am pretty sure that all the others in there are Guests, and not Humans. They are putting things into a big bag, and so I expect they will come out soon. I am very sad to think that I won't be able to talk to Lorna, but at least I will be able to follow her for a while. How long I can follow her for depends on where she goes.

I think they are just leaving the Cabin. I come out from behind the tree and run round to the front of the Cabin. This is quite risky but I have no choice if I am going to be able to follow her. They are heading for the Village Green. Damn. That means they are going somewhere I can't follow: probably Splashdown. I can't get into Splashdown. I knew something like this would happen.

*

'Mum?'

'Yes, child?'

'Can I get some swimming clothes?'

'You don't need clothes to swim in the lake. You can just go naked when there are no Guests around.'

'Mm. Yes. Well. I want some swimming clothes.'

'What kind of "swimming clothes"?'

'Like they have in the shop by the Village Green.'

4

'You mean that place frequented by Guests?'

'Er, yes.'

'That place of Sin and Iniquity? You want to go in there, and be discovered, and lead Them to our Sacred Home, so that we would be cast out? Is that what you want? To be cast into Outer Darkness?'

'Oh, never mind.'

'Child! Come back here!'

But I had gone by then. She realised that she was shouting. She goes mad with me if I shout. She might have thought about running after me, but she didn't. I had a good start on her, and she knows I am faster at running than she is, especially through the forest.

*

I stole some swimming shorts off the washing line at the back of Cabin Y29 and they fit me really well. They have a strange pattern on them, and some Guest writing which I can't understand. It has the same letters as the Litany, but I don't understand what it says. My mother would probably tell me that it is something to do with Sinfulness, but she has not seen them.

Lorna and I are inside Splashdown. Nobody has noticed that I am Human. Nobody seems bothered about me at all, except Lorna. We are sitting in a bubbling pool of warm water. It is just the two of us. The pool is big enough for about eight, but there is no-one else here. The water is so warm that I felt as if my body was going to melt at first, but I have got used to it, now. Lorna and I are holding hands under the water. Her swimming clothes are very revealing. She has small bumps on her chest that I can't stop looking at. I wish we could stay here forever. I have not had anything to eat today, but I don't feel hungry. I feel as if I won't need to eat again, as long as I can stay next to Lorna. She is speaking to me again.

'Orion, what are we going to do when I have to go home?'

'You mean you can't stay here?'

'No, of course not, silly. We are going home in two days.' I didn't know what to say. I wanted to say, '*But you are a Human and so, as soon as you leave, you will be cast into Outer Darkness.*' But I didn't. I knew that Lorna would not believe me. I could not believe that Lorna's life was about to end. It just did not seem to make sense.

Now the Guest man from Lorna's Cabin has come over and is talking to Lorna. She keeps hold of my hand under the water. The bubbles mean that he can't see what we are doing. Lorna has to go and get dry and go back to the Cabin. I follow her, to get a few more minutes with her.

Lorna's Guest woman asks me a lot of questions, just like my mother would expect her to.

'Where are your mum and dad, Orion?'

'My mother is at home.'

'And where's your dad?'

'I don't know.'

'Oh. Do you mean your mother is at your Cabin?'

'Er. Yes. She's at the Cabin. It's D14.' I deliberately thought of a Cabin that was as far from Lorna's as you could get.

'Aren't you a bit young to be coming here and getting changed and swimming on your own?'

'I'm a very good swimmer. My mother says I need to learn to look after myself.'

'Oh, does she?' We finished getting dry. I thought that would be the end of my day with Lorna, but the Guest woman asked me if I wanted to go back to their Cabin.

*

Lorna's family are getting ready to leave. I arranged to meet her on Pirate Island, very early. I suppose we have had quite a long time together, but now she has to go. She kisses me. I have never been kissed by anyone except my mother. She turns to go, and I feel as if my insides are about to fall out onto the floor. I can't start crying, because my mother will want to know why I'm upset and I'll never hear the end of it. In my trouser pocket, I have a piece of paper with instructions on which Lorna gave to me. She says we can contact each other by using Guest Sorcery called the Internet. I know there are Sorcery Machines in the American Diner which people use for this.

After Lorna had left, I went up to the Border and climbed over the fence. I walked around a bit outside, in the Outer Darkness. Nothing happened. It was no different from in here really, except there were fewer trees.

*

Last winter was terrible. It was so cold that my mother and I left our home for a while and broke into a Cabin to keep warm. Most of the Keepers go away for about thirty days each winter, and we stayed until about the time they came back. When there are no Keepers, there are no Guests, and no Guests means less food. We had to eat squirrels. It was revolting at first, but after a few weeks, I was catching as many of them as I could.

It is May now. I have been staying in touch with Lorna by what she tells me I should call 'instant messaging'. She is coming back next month. She says she can't wait to see me again.

be right back

Briggsy showed me an instant message he had just received from Sarah, who was sitting at the other side of the office.

hello how would you like to bend me over your desk and

fuck me really hard??

'What do you think of that?' he asked.

'I think it is a bulletin from the Office of Too Much Information.'

There are so many women called Sarah in Briggsy's life that I have introduced a numbering system. Sarah Number One, also known as 'Squeak', is a wannabe web designer who lives in Briggsy's old flat in Sheffield. She is the person you usually get if you call Briggsy's mobile. Sarah Number Two, the love of Briggsy's life, threw him out of the house about five years ago, and now won't have anything to do with him. She is the woman he thinks of when he stares into his drink. Sarah Number Three is a hairdresser from Rotherham with two children. The children like Briggsy but, at the moment, Sarah Number Three does not. Sarah Number Four is the one in the office who likes it from behind. I am in-between relationships at the moment. I have split up with Clarisse, my wife, in the sense that we are getting a divorce and have completely separate lives, but we still live under the same roof.

Briggsy and I are members of the same internet dating site. He gets far more dates than I do, and usually with much more desirable women, even though he is unshaven, full of self-loathing, cannot cook, has never been to university, and owns next to nothing apart from a black bin-liner full of his army trophies. Most of the messages I get are either from women in Eastern Europe who speak poor English and who want money, or women in West Africa who speak no English and who want a husband and right of domicile in the EU. I must say that the West African women are certainly helping me to brush up my French. Through a combination of what I learnt at school and judicious use of Google Translate (I am a fast typist) I can manage to hold quite an advanced conversation, for all the good it does me.

At the moment I am corresponding with a woman who refuses to meet me. She goes by the name of 'Lady Scarlet'. We seem to have uncannily similar tastes in music. I told Briggsy everything I have managed to find out about her, and realised when I got to the end that it had taken less than a minute. Every time I ask her a detailed question about her work, or try to move the conversation in the direction of an arrangement to meet, she goes offline.

*

Now Briggsy is showing me a text message. It is from Gemma, a psychiatric nurse in Rotherham with whom he is sleeping but not having a relationship.

> Please can the early morning sex reach climax before 6.30
>
> in future? I am exhausted after running for the train. Nearly
>
> missed the bleeder.
>
> xXXx

He then shows me a picture he took of her. The picture shows her from collar-bone to mid-thigh, and she is naked. Her figure is slightly fuller than Briggsy's usual preference. There is no way of telling from the picture whether it was taken with or without the subject's knowledge or consent.

I have no pictures of Lady Scarlet. She does not even use an avatar which is obviously fake, such as a picture of Wonder Woman or a furry gonk. She says she is tall, curvy and has red hair and blue eyes. In combination with the fact that she is a lawyer and likes ska, punk and new wave music, this makes her sound too good to be true. She might be too good to be true if it weren't for the fact that she is difficult to communicate with and so far will not agree to meet me.

'Do Gemma and Sarah Number Four know about each other?' I ask him. He looks at me as if I am an idiot. Neither of them has asked about the other, and this is why he has not told them. Briggsy does not consider that he is doing anything dishonest. Just then, he receives a text message from Sarah Number Three, who seems to want to see him again. Briggsy has spent the last few nights back in Sheffield, being looked after by Sarah Number One. She gave him smoked haddock for his tea last night, and now he is complaining of stomach pains. I think she is trying to poison him, but Briggsy won't see it. He seems to think Sarah Number One is incapable of any malign intent.

*

Clarisse is arranging to go and stay with her parents at the weekend. This is an exciting prospect for me. It will clear the house of the emotional atmosphere which pervades it when we are both at home. It will enable me to drink alcohol without attracting disapproval, and it will also allow me to have internet chat with Lady Scarlet in private. She tends to be online quite late, usually around midnight. If the conversation goes on a long time, it can be difficult for me to get enough sleep and have eliminated the alcohol from my system before Clarisse, who has the most sensitive nose of any human being I have ever known, gets home on Sunday afternoon. I have taken to making a big steaming pan of curry for Sunday lunch, and Clarisse has not yet begun to suspect why this is. She gratefully eats up the leftovers.

Clarisse and I have one of those warm and civilised conversations which, taken in isolation, would make you wonder why we are splitting up.

'I am taking my human rights textbook to Barnsley with me.'

'Because you are worried about the impending collapse of civil society in that part of the world.'

'No – silly.'

She hovers around the hall, endlessly re-checking her luggage. I eventually hear the door slam, the car start and the engine noise diminish as she drives away. We are past the point in our relationship where a door slamming on its own would signify anything – it could have been a ruse. I get into my car and drive the four hundred yards to the off-licence. Clarisse virtually banned alcohol about three years ago when we started the first of five failed courses of IVF. Valuable seconds of drinking time are now ticking away and I don't want to waste any of them.

Back in front of my PC, I am drinking lager with ice in it because the shop's fridge had just been restocked. There is some vodka – the remains of a quarter bottle that I keep in the one hiding place that Clarisse has never discovered (inside the oven gloves) – but I don't want to get drunk too quickly. Chatting with Lady Scarlet requires tact and diplomacy as well as confidence, and so no more than a moderate state of inebriation is required. I pass some time by reading through my other messages (which takes about two minutes) and popping out for a Chinese meal. The restaurant is also at the end of the road. Clarisse and I have lived here for seven years, and she has never set foot in the place, even though she eats Chinese food. I take my phone with me, and while I am waiting for my chicken and sweetcorn soup to cool, I exchange text messages with Briggsy. He is drinking, smoking dope, and playing a game on his Xbox. His stomach pains have gone away but he still does not feel like going out. I wish I had Lady Scarlet's mobile phone number.

I manage to spin the meal out almost until the *Jade Palace* closes, which means that by the time I get home, Lady Scarlet should be about to come online. After drinking a bottle of white wine with my dinner, I must be a bit drunker than I think I am, because I notice that the laurel bushes on the traffic island in the middle of the street are densely foliated, and decide to hide inside them to have a piss. I can hear Clarisse's voice inside my head.

'That's a criminal offence, that is. It doesn't matter whether anybody saw you or not: that's indecent exposure. As long as you exposed yourself in such a way that, had there been anybody there, they might have seen you, that is indecent exposure.' She is not a criminal lawyer, but that is what she would have said. That is one of the reasons I enjoy pissing in unusual places.

I am delighted to find that Lady Scarlet is online and the lager is now acceptably cold. Unusually, she initiates the conversation by sending me a message shortly after I sign in. She addresses me by my online pseudonym.

Hello Aubrey. What are you doing at the moment?

Typing.

Silly. What are you really doing?

Listening to an album by "The Beat".

Oh, The Beat always remind me of my teenage years. Where did those good times go? Which album is it?

I Just Can't Stop It.

I know you really like listening to them, but which album is it?

The album is called "I Just Can't Stop It". Couldn't you tell from the capitalisation?

Oh, of course. Sorry. I keep forgetting that you are very correct with typing, even in an instant message conversation.

Yes, I am weird like that. Have you made up your mind about a meeting yet?

I don't want to meet yet. I'm still nervous.

Why is that?

I have come out of a very bad relationship recently. Men still cause me deep anxiety.

OK. I understand.

I think I need to build up confidence gradually, in little installments.

At least she doesn't go offline this time, which is what she has done on every previous occasion that I have asked any such question. I don't bother to mention to her that it is unusual for someone versed in English law to spell the word 'instalments' with two Ls. I don't want to sound like a geek. After three cans of lager and a whole bottle of wine, my bladder is rapidly filling, but I don't want to type "be right back" and drop the conversation, even for a minute. If I don't keep going, Lady Scarlet may decide to go offline and I have no idea how I would spend the rest of the night. I recently mentioned that I go to a therapist, and it did not scare her away.

I have started to feel more confident about meeting people since I started going to the therapist.

That's good. Why do you think it has helped?

I think I feel more confident in my ability to understand other people's feelings. My estranged wife is convinced that I suffer from Asperger's syndrome.

Why do you think she says that?

I am not really sure. She reeled off a list of the symptoms that she thinks I suffer from, and I listened to it as sympathetically as I could, but to me they were simply the characteristics of masculinity — nothing to do with any syndrome.

Give me an example of one of the things she said.

Being emotionally distant.

I am not so sure that is a characteristic that all men share.

12

I am. Certainly all straight men. Probably a lot of gay men, too.

Do you think being emotionally distant contributed to the break-up of your marriage?

I am sure it did, but it was not all my fault.

What do you blame your wife for?

All the unreasonable things she did, and the fact that she was never, ever happy or satisfied. This divorce is the first amicable thing we have ever jointly embarked on. The therapist suspects she may have personality disorder.

it is very unprofessional of the therapist to discuss a third party with you.

She is not a 'third party' – she is my estranged wife. It would be impossible for me to have a sensible conversation with the therapist without mentioning her.

Well I think it is unprofessional. And you should not have told me about it. I think you are indiscrete.

You mean indiscreet. Indiscrete means something else.

There you go again. You are always trying to divert attention from the real problem, and the real problem is you. I think you need much more therapy.

What makes you think I intend ever to stop going to therapy? I get all the therapy I can afford to pay for.

Well I think you need more intensive therapy.

'So does Clarisse,' I thought. And then it hit me. I instantly closed the chat window. The earlier promise that the evening had showed evaporated in an instant. I assembled the evidence in my mind.

Lady Scarlet is only ever online when Clarisse is out of the house. There was one occasion when that meant only just out of the house (in the car, sitting in the drive) but Clarisse has a smartphone and she could have used that. They are both lawyers, but Lady Scarlet would not give me any details about where she worked or any cases. This explained how Clarisse seemed to anticipate every nuance of my taste in music – that was the lure she had used to attract my interest. But it was the characteristics of her typing that clinched it. Both Clarisse and

13

Lady Scarlet had used the rather unusual words "installment" and "indiscrete", and spelt them in exactly the same incorrect way. The vituperative tone was now unmistakably recognisable.

What I resented was having Lady Scarlet taken away from me. Talking to her had been the high point of my week.

When Clarisse arrived home on Sunday afternoon, there was a momentary flash of recognition in her eyes as I watched her enter the house, but that was all. She admitted nothing, even when I presented her with all the evidence. I never spoke to Lady Scarlet again, and she never spoke to me.

Sarah Number Four asked Briggsy for a date on a night when he was seeing Gemma, which happened to be her (Sarah's) birthday. She surmised from his evasive replies that he was seeing someone else. She got upset and finished with him. He has started seeing Sarah Number Three again. He showed me a naked picture of her on his phone. She would kill him if she found out he had done that.

Your Writing Thing

My name is Patrick Spencer. I am the first person narrator of this story. I am starting *in medias res*, in a pub in the railway station in Leeds. I am not sure what the pub is called, because I am not omniscient. Since I have drawn attention to the fact that I am telling you a story, we can call this a narrative 'from the inside'. It is in the present tense. As to genre, you can decide that for yourself. There will be no magic or vampires. I am sick of all that stuff.

I am wondering whether to tell you how I got here, or whether to leave that as back story. Yes: I'll tell you. I had been invited back to Leeds by an old university friend who was having a party. This was in full swing when a wall bracket failed and a Wharfedale speaker hit my host on the head. The corner of the wooden casing split his scalp open and he bled copiously. He fell unconscious and a few other guests started screaming when they realised they had been spattered with blood. He had to be taken to hospital with a suspected fractured skull, and I had to leave his flat a day earlier than planned. My return ticket to London had been booked in advance and I could not afford to buy another.

That was how I came to have a full English breakfast in this pub, and a pint of bitter at 11:00 a.m. It is now 11:30 (let's get back into the present tense and being *in medias res* as quickly as possible). I am just having another pint.

I take out my small notebook (a plain 3½ by 5½-inch Moleskine, naturally) and I try to make the most of the situation. I work for the marketing department of a London-based bookseller. I studied English with Creative Writing at university, but the writing habit left me as soon as I started full-time work. In the last couple of years, I have been trying to force myself to get back into it. I now carry my notebook wherever I go.

I am jotting down fragments about the brown, wooden interior of the bar – semi-colon – about the jaded-looking staff, pre-programmed to ask you with every pint if you want any crisps or peanuts, and, of course, the other patrons. I catalogue three specimens: a thin, elderly man who looks longingly at an empty Guinness glass; a man with a shaved head and green Harrington jacket who assiduously studies the racing pages of his newspaper, and a large lady with big, bleached blonde hair, a bright red coat and four department store shopping bags, who talks animatedly in a soft Scouse accent into her mobile phone. I conduct this study as discreetly as I can. I don't want the first one to ask me for money. I don't want the second one to punch me, and I don't want the third one to try to talk to me. I now turn to the remaining one. He turns to me, at the same time. He also has a pen in his hand, and a small notebook – not a Moleskine – on the table in front of him, next to his pint and two empty glasses.

I am certainly not looking in a mirror. My co-observer looks at least fifty-five, with lank, grey hair that needs cutting, two days' beard growth, a V-neck woollen jumper gone at both elbows, a denim shirt that is too small and reveals a tuft of white chest-hair, blue twill trousers with one hem coming down, and grimy tennis shoes that look as if they came from a market stall. He has a few belongings on the chair next to him in a supermarket carrier-bag.

We idly blink at each other, and put our pens down. I hear someone speak. I am speaking.

'Do you want another drink?'

'Cheers.' An awkward pause. He pushes a foam-clouded glass towards me. 'Since you're buying, I'll have a pint of John Smith's and a large Bell's, please.' I scan the table in front of him, and the two tables next to him for either a tumbler or a ring which might be evidence of a tumbler. There is none. Despite being overfed, temporarily displaced and having had two pints before midday, I still have a decision to make. Am I content to fork out three pounds fifty for a large whisky that he would not pay for himself?

I go to the bar and get two pints of bitter and the whisky.

'Are you a writer?' he asks, as I sit down again.

'Not yet. Are you?'

'I write some short fiction. Mostly I run a fortnightly writing competition on a website called "Your Writing Thing".'

'Oh?' I must have succeeded in looking blank, because a shadow of disappointment falls across his face, but I know exactly what he is talking about. I spend every other Sunday afternoon waiting for this competition to start. I have entered it fifty-one times so far. I have never won it. I have never been in the top three.

16

He takes a mouthful of beer and another of whisky. I glance at my watch, mainly to gauge how degenerate we are being by drinking this much alcohol this early in the day.

'What time's your train?' he asks.

'Not for a while yet. Yours?' Mine is in fact in twenty-two hours and thirty-eight minutes.

'I'm not waiting for a train.'

'Well if you're not a traveller, and you don't look like a trainspotter, what are you doing here?'

'I'm blocked. I quite often come here when I'm blocked.'

I am still trying to work out why I bought this man a drink when I realise that I am about to say to him the very thing that he most wants to hear.

'Tell me about "Your Writing Thing".' Before he replies, he displays a strange mannerism by which his head shakes from side-to-side a few times, he shivers, and then taps his fingertips on the tabletop. He takes several gulps from both his drinks.

'Each competition is based on prompts: one prop (an object), the name of one character (say "A man called 'Trevor'"), and one location.' He drones on about the format of the competition, and I stop listening. I already know how it works. I have studied the rubric on the home page until I know it off by heart. I have read as much as I can about the regular winners. I descend into a reverie of alcohol and railway station background noise, which is the best way of not registering how desperate I am to win "Your Writing Thing", how much I want to be able to put that achievement on my literary CV as preparation for getting an agent or a publisher. I resurface just as he starts to describe what has recently gone wrong with his venture.

'I was convinced that "Your Writing Thing" would make money. I thought it would be more popular than it is, and I thought I could push it through what I have heard called "the inverse pricing pyramid" – that means that I thought I would be able to increase the subscription price and still go on increasing the number of subscribers: get it to acquire snob-value, in other words. I was hoping that eventually it would land me a way back into at least a temporary lectureship at a university which teaches creative writing. I was also hoping that some of the regular contributors, the more talented ones, might engage me to act as their agent.' He pauses for a moment to

17

wring out one of the torn cuffs of his jumper which he has just realised has been dipping into his beer. 'I find it quite vexing that the better writers among my regular competitors also seem to be competent at marketing themselves. I had been hoping for a nice, stable-but-socially-inept genius somewhere along the way, but no such luck.

'And, of course, I was hoping to sell advertising on the website. That produces some income, but only a trickle. It didn't even go down at the start of the Credit Crunch, because it was so low to start with.' He pauses, takes a long draught of beer and finishes his whisky. He pushes the glass towards me, but I remain seated while he carries on talking.

'Recently, things have been so bad that I have started to supplement my income – how shall I put it – illegitimately.'

'What?'

' "Your Writing Thing" became a bent website.'

I stare at him. I want to say, 'Bent in what way?' He looks at me expectantly before continuing.

'First of all, I invented five fictitious competitors. They are called Judy Blackhill, Imelda Casey, Winnie Riding, Tom Norton, and Rosemary Drinkwater. One of them wins nearly every week's competition. I actually start the year now by setting up a spreadsheet which tells me when each of them is going to win, be runner-up, or come third. That saves me a total of a hundred quid every fortnight in prize money.

'Judy Blackhill writes about crimes of passion in very mundane, domestic settings. Her art is mainly in the build-up, and applying a twist, or sometimes two, to the story. Imelda Casey is a creator of evocative and unusual settings. Her stories tend to take place on top of skyscrapers, or mountains, or in laboratories or observatories, or in houses on stilts over tropical rivers. Winnie Riding churns out historical stuff, often involving gulfs in social standing and some sexual undertones (though never anything explicit). Tom Norton produces psychological dramas set among city investors, politicians, or officers in HM forces. Rosemary Drinkwater puts all her main characters through an emotional wringer. The hero or heroine always ends up by destroying the person or thing he or she loves, either deliberately or accidentally. She might sound a bit like Judy Blackhill, but her characters live in much posher houses, smash more expensive crockery, and one of the characters is sometimes a horse or a pony.

'What I do after each competition has closed is to read through the entries – not all of them, obviously: most of them are an embarrassing load of crap – I mean the entries from the more talented regulars, and pick out any ideas which might be publishable. I then polish them up a bit at my leisure, and submit them to some of the magazines I have been cultivating, all under pen-names, of course.'

'What is your name, by the way?' He looks at me as if I might be from the Inland Revenue, but does eventually reply.

'Neil Bartram.' That is the name I recognise from the website. I wonder if I might ever have heard of any of the pseudonyms he uses to steal other people's ideas, but I do not ask him about them. He starts tapping the table again.

'My main source of material recently has been a bloke called Philip Lumb. He writes mostly about infidelity, intrigue and clashes of personality among academics. "Professor Plum" I call him. He has a wife, called Elvira, who can't punctuate or spell and who has taken to sending me messages of complaint from the Prof's email address. I thought at first that he might have a split personality, but that would be too good to be true. She seems to be a genuinely and very tediously devoted spouse. Every time I open one of her missives, I can smell the hearty casserole and the freshly-cut flowers. Elvira rants about how good Plum's latest entry is, and how appalled she is that it didn't win anything. I awarded him a second prize recently – cost me thirty quid, that did – but it didn't placate her. She said it only went to show how inconsistent the judging was, because the one I had short-listed was nowhere near his best. There is no pleasing some people.' He stops talking and gazes at his empty glasses. We both need the toilet. I wait until Neil has come back before I make my own visit. Something about being in the toilet with him seems repellent, especially if he were to carry on talking. I buy another round. I am wondering just how much money he has misappropriated from Philip Lumb, and the others, and what he does with the proceeds. I am wondering if any of my own stories have been good enough to steal. I enter the competition under the name "Caleb Vickers".

Neil takes an A4 pad out of his carrier bag, and starts goading me to pick one of his five ghost writers, so that he can produce seven hundred words in his or her style, there and then, but I don't bite. I know their styles: I have studied them. I have a whole notebook at home which is devoted to emulating them. I finish my drink and get out. I walk a long way and turn down as many side streets as I can before selecting another pub.

*

Neil Bartram and I are in the pub again, but a year has passed, and we are in London. Caleb Vickers has now entered "Your Writing Thing" seventy-two times, and achieved one third place. Earlier, Neil and I were in my company's Oxford Street branch, attending a reading given by Philip Lumb. His first novel was recently published. It is called *Delicate Instruments*. Fortunately, Elvira Lumb was not present.

Before the beginning of the question and answer session, I had not noticed Neil. His hand went up first and Vicki, my boss, who does not know Neil, picked him. Ten minutes later, he was asked to leave because he was being deliberately offensive to Philip. Vicki told me to stay with "that nutter who looks like a homeless guy" until the event was over. I have just looked at my watch. I have to mind him for another thirty-four minutes. I have paid for the round, again. Conversation does not flow.

'He'll get better, I suppose, eventually. Perhaps. Professor Plum, I mean.' says Neil.

'Why are you so disparaging about Philip Lumb's writing?'

'Oh, come on. There are characters and incidents mentioned in the first chapter that are never picked up or resolved. There are vital pieces of information which are just foisted on the reader without development or suspense. There is dialogue that doesn't do anything, other than fill the page. Need I go on?'

'Is your first novel selling well? Did you drink a lot of wine at the launch party?' He ignores me.

'I'm not letting him win a prize in "Your Writing Thing" again after this. I'll tell you that for nothing. Not after getting me thrown out of his precious signing session.'

'In the first place, it was Vicki, my boss, who ordered you to be removed. Secondly, Vicki's action was reasonable and humane because every other member of the audience was dying of embarrassment because of your inflammatory remarks. Thirdly – and most importantly – I have noticed how, every time you talk about the writing competition you run, your discussion of the outcome and the awarding of prizes has nothing at all to do with the quality of the pieces written by the competitors.' Neil ignores me again. I have just thought of a way to get his attention: all I have to do is buy a drink for myself and not for him. I sip a large whisky and he looks at me as if what I am doing is scandalous, aberrant and preventable. I remember that, inside my wallet is the cheque for ten pounds he sent me for coming third in the competition. The cheque is now out of date. I never attempted to cash it because he had not signed it. 'I am grateful to you for one thing,' I tell him.

'And what might that be?'

'Since I began seriously trying to be a writer, I have changed, because of having met you. Previously, I hankered after all literary acquaintances. Anyone who had had so much as one or two pieces published in magazines was more established than me and hence, as I foolishly thought, possessed of celebrity. Since I met you, I have realised that there are people who smell of books and manuscripts, who look and sound like writers, but whose careers are not going anywhere, mostly because they can't write for toffee.'

'I've had plenty of pieces published.'

'Yes, but you admitted to me that you got the ideas for most of those by plagiarism. Why do you make things so difficult? Why all this intrigue and exploitation of other people? Why don't you just do what the rest of us do? Keep a notebook. Cultivate the writing habit. Do some preparation, and then sit down and write something. Keep a file of all your rejection slips. Persevere. Be professional.'

'The market's changed. That old-fashioned stuff doesn't work any more.'

'How the hell do you know? You've never tried it.' I look at my watch again.

'Is Professor Plum's moment of glory over now?'

'His name is Philip Lumb. Why can't you call him by his name? This evening's reading, in our flagship London branch, is indeed over now. Tomorrow he reads in Southampton. Then on to Bristol, Cardiff, Birmingham, Nottingham, Lincoln, Leeds, Manchester, Liverpool, Newcastle, Glasgow and Edinburgh. Not bad for a start. I spoke to Philip before the reading – he is a very personable chap – and I congratulate him for having done a clever thing. He has already written his second novel. I don't think he will be entering "Your Writing Thing" again.' I don't think Caleb Vickers will, either.

I finish my drink and walk out of the pub without saying another word. I had to leave to stop myself from asking Neil his opinion of the submissions from Caleb Vickers. I go straight home, make a cup of tea, and do *my* writing thing: two thousand words of short fiction before bed (first person narrator, present tense, contemporary and realistic setting) and I set the alarm for five-thirty so that first thing tomorrow I can do some morning pages.

I can't help re-visiting and retrospectively re-phrasing my conversation with Neil as I try to go to sleep. I said at the beginning that there wouldn't be any vampires in this. I am sorry: there was one.

How to be an Alcoholic

The most important thing is to start gradually. Alcohol is wasted on the young. Get a decent education. Go to a respected university. Don't start until at least after you have taken your finals.

Do not, on any account, mix it with other drugs. In spite of the claims made by nicotine, heroin, cocaine, or cannabis, alcohol is the only drug you will ever need. It is legal, affordable, socially acceptable (mostly), and, if you want it to be, addictive.

Let us not get into an argument about whether absinthe counts as alcohol, or as something else. All we will say is that absinthe would not be nearly as fashionable at the moment if it weren't 55 per cent alcohol by volume.

As with most things, the secret is in preparation and dedication. You will need a reason to drink. Work is the most obvious one. Get a job. Any job. But preferably one in which your co-workers drink. Become a "social" drinker. That is, a drinker who drinks in the same room as, and at the same time as, other people.

During your twenties, you will probably find that your consumption is curtailed as much by financial constraints as by your own capacity. You will also find that you spend a certain amount of time throwing up into toilets, or gutters, or sinks. This is a terrible waste, but don't worry about it, because you will get over it, later. It's just a phase.

At about thirty, you will need another reason to drink. The most obvious is a bad relationship. It doesn't matter whether you are gay or straight: find a partner who is either deliberately or inadvertently trying to destroy you, and vow to stick with him or her, whatever happens.

If you have been careful, it is not until this point that you will be accused of having a drink problem. There are various ways of mitigating this. For a year or two, you should be able to manage only drinking a few days per week, or only drinking relatively low-alcohol drinks, such as beer. Once you have exhausted these techniques, you are ready to move onto the next stage, which is concealing alcohol. This is a graduation in your development, and probably the biggest since you started drinking.

The only limits to concealing alcohol are the dimensions of your house and the fertility of your imagination. It is tempting at first only to try to conceal spirits, because they are more concentrated, but that is missing the point.

That bottle of Ribena at the back of the cupboard that nobody has touched for three years could be emptied and refilled with port. That over-filled spice-cupboard could be augmented with a couple of bottles of Chinese cooking wine (13 per cent ABV) which are unlikely to be noticed and, even if they are, might legitimately be there as cooking wine. It helps if you altruistically promote the habit of going to the supermarket by yourself, and also if you keep the old, gunge-coated bottles, and refill them from the new ones. If you have got this far, you will already have established yourself as the partner who does all the cooking. The kitchen is your domain, in more than one way.

The kitchen is not only the place where much of your consumption takes place, but also where you carry out many of your concealment activities. For example, a partner who never cooks is unlikely ever – even after an incident – to be interested in oven gloves. An oven glove will easily accommodate a quarter bottle of vodka, and makes a much safer point of concealment than a shelf in a study or bedroom, or at the back of a clothes drawer.

Have no compunction about cleaning up your own vomit, or admitting to the therapist what you have drunk, when, and why.

Once the relationship which turned you into a serious drinker is over, you are ready for the next step.

You need to learn to drink just for the sake of drinking. How you do this is up to you. It is likely during this period that you may decide more than once that you want to stop drinking. Stay with it.

Case study:

I moved into a house with Caroline and Jacob and the kitchen was too small and the bathroom had no shower and so we built an extension. The builders demolished the garage and built out across the drive and we got an extra bedroom and a bigger bathroom with a walk-in shower and a bidet and downstairs a utility room for the washing machine and vented tumble dryer and I was wondering where we were going to put the litter tray for Caroline's cats when she told me she and Jacob were moving out.

I sit on the new sofa in the extension. This area is too cold. This area doesn't have enough radiators. This area doesn't have enough plug sockets. What do you want plug sockets here for they said. I said mobile phone chargers, laptops, Kindle chargers, battery-chargers, and anything else that somebody might invent. I didn't bother to say portable electric heaters. They said no. I was angry because I have built an extension before and it didn't have enough plug sockets. I know about plug sockets and radiators. There aren't enough in this extension.

It is time for me to put my walking boots on and walk to the filling-station. I could get to the filling-station much quicker if I drove there in my car, but that would not be a good idea. It only takes about nine minutes to walk to the filling-station. Of course, it takes about nine minutes to walk back again from the filling-station, but it only takes about nine minutes to get there.

There are two ways to get out of my house. I usually go out of the front door, but this time I decide to go out of the patio door at the back. I unlock the patio door. I turn the patio lights on. I open the door. I step through the door. I come back in again and turn the patio lights off. I leave the door ajar, because I can.

I walk to the filling-station.

I select a bottle of Argentinian Carmenère. I would prefer the Malbec, but the Carmenère is two pounds cheaper. I select a bottle of Sauvignon Blanc which is slightly above my usual price range. I select two bottles of Indian lager which are on special offer.

There is no queue. As I place my basket down, I ask for a half-bottle of Smirnoff. I pay with my debit card.

This is about the eleventh time I have gone out with the patio door open.

The first, second and third times, nothing happened.

The fourth, fifth, and sixth times, I found a cat on my kitchen counter, looking for food. It was a ginger cat which sprayed piss. I had to clean the kitchen with bleach.

The seventh, eighth, ninth, and tenth times, nothing happened.

There might have been another time.

Having let myself out through the patio doors at the back, so that I could drop some bottles into the recycling bin, I return through the front. I don't remember having left the lights on.

'Hello, John,' someone says.

'Hello, Scott,' someone else says. That is me.

'What are you doing here?' says Scott.

'I live here. What are you doing here?'

'I was hoping I might be able to stay here for a while.' That question is typical of Scott. I hate Scott. He leaves toast crumbs in the margarine. He takes hours and hours in the bathroom, and he leaves damp towels everywhere. He insists on having the television on all day, whether he is watching it or not. He uses food, soap, shampoo, shaving foam, deodorant, detergent, and every consumable you can think of, except salt. He brings his own salt, which he broadcasts widely over the sofa and the carpet, every time he sprinkles it.

I think it is the salt that does it. Somehow, I get him to move out. I can't remember how I do it, or how long it takes. All I can remember is that the neighbours complain.

I am drinking white wine from the off-licence, for the fourth night in a row. Tomorrow starts in one hour and fifteen minutes, and is Tuesday, a work day, but this is only week 1 and so I don't have to do much other than sign in.

I have fleas. I have had fleas since the last of Caroline's cats moved out. I sit on the upstairs toilet and watch the fleas jump onto my legs. I spray a bit of eau de toilette onto the bidet, which is next to the toilet, and then I pinch the flea between my thumb and forefinger. If you press a flea onto a surface covered in eau de toilette, it can't jump away. I think it must be the alcohol. It goes into a stupor, and then dies. I'm killing them at an average of about six or seven a day. I think the record for one day is twelve. It is either twelve or twenty-two.

I go to bed.

I wake up. I don't bother to set an alarm. If I did, I would probably sleep through it. Eventually, I get up.

I sit on the sofa in the kitchen-dining area downstairs, either in my dressing gown, or with my trousers rolled up, and I watch fleas jump onto my legs. Because the eau de toilette is upstairs, I destroy them with my fingernails. You pinch it at first and get it between your

26

thumb and forefinger. Then you get it under your thumbnail. And then you bring up a fingernail, so that it gets caught between the hammer and the anvil. You can see the legs fanning out as you flatten it. It is easy to tell the difference between a live flea and one that has been destroyed. They are piling up on the floor. I wonder what eats dead fleas. Some kind of spider, possibly. I am not afraid of spiders. I have stopped cutting my fingernails. I have two pairs of nail scissors, and I know exactly where both of them are. I still cut my toenails, sometimes. Toenails are no use for killing fleas.

The problem is while I am asleep. I tend to pass out, which means that the fleas get to drink warm Bloody Mary all night, on tap from me. When I wake up, I inspect my lower legs. What I am looking for is pale pink spots. That means recent flea bites. I released poison gas in my bedroom a few weeks ago, but it doesn't seem to have cured the problem. I check my phone and my emails to make sure nothing has exploded at work, and then I run the bath. At least I have a tiled bathroom with a walk-in shower, a bath that is big enough for two, basin, toilet, bidet and towel dryer. I can't afford to pay for it, but it is still mine, for now. I have given up on Molton Brown bath bubbles, because I can't afford eighteen quid for a bottle. I buy Radox from the Co-op. It isn't as good, but I put up with it.

I wash my lower legs, especially the areas that have started to bleed or suppurate because I have scratched them. I don't want to go septic. That would not do at all. I make sure to put plenty of soap suds on those areas. The warm water makes the new bites itch unbearably, and so I scratch both legs alternately for a long time, from my heels to my knees. While I am in the bath, it doesn't matter if some of the bites start to bleed.

There is cricket on the radio: a test match. I kick myself for having slept in beyond 11 o'clock.

I look for my spectacles. If they are on the chest of drawers next to the bed, or the window ledge in the bathroom, that probably means that I knew what I was doing when I went to bed the previous night. If they are under a sofa or in the fridge, it probably means I did not.

I put the kettle on. I take 40 milligrams of fluoxetine, sometimes with water and sometimes with the remains of a glass of wine. Sometimes I have remembered to put the wine glass in the fridge before I go to bed. Sometimes I haven't. I make tea. I make two cups, including one in Caroline's old lady's cup, as if she were still here. I add sugar if I have a hangover. I drink the tea.

I log on again and I find that something has happened at work. I start to deal with it. I'm actually working. I know what I'm doing and I'm good at it. It is too complicated to explain what I do.

I have put LED bulbs in the bathroom. It is cheaper, because I never turn that light off. At least there is one light that never goes out. I've had a letter from work and another which looks like it is from the police. I don't know when I am going to open them. The police one might be something to do with the car.

When all the work stuff is over, I still have some white wine and some lager left, and two of my friends are online.

Something I Need to Tell You

Mm. I love getting ready to see Aubrey. First, I have a nice, long, bath. Nice and warm but not hot, and plenty of expensive bubbles. Molton Brown Blissful Templetree is Aubrey's favourite, and it always reminds me of that bath we had together in that fantastic suite at Mal Maison on Deansgate. That was one of the three over-nighters we have had. Three over-nighters with the same client in about three months. Not bad. For each one, I offered him a discount: £450 instead of £600 and, of course, Aubrey being such a gentleman, he gave me at least £600 anyway, every time.

I wish I knew more about where he gets his money from. I wish I knew how much he earns. I don't think his house is anything special. He has never taken me there. And he never mentions having an au pair, or a gardener, or horses, or more than one car. He owns a flat somewhere, but I think it is rented to some poor person. He is such a kind man. One of the kindest men I have ever known. He has bought me presents a few times, and I'm not talking just a box of Belgian truffles or a bottle of bubbly: I mean serious jewellery. He bought me a pair of diamond studs that must have been half a carat each – at least. I'm never going to sell them. I am going to keep them forever.

In the bath, I shave my legs, but not down there. Aubrey doesn't like that. And I put my most expensive underwear on (usually something that Aubrey has bought me), and something fairly figure-hugging but elegant and with classical lines. Aubrey loves my figure. Every time I tell him I am on a diet or have been to the gym, he tells me I don't need to. I don't always wear the jewellery he has given me. Aubrey is not the sort of client to inspect me to see if I am wearing something he has bought. He is really mild-tempered, and not at all possessive. He is really understanding when I open up to him about the stress I am having with my other clients. I love looking at myself in the mirror as I am getting dressed and ready to meet Aubrey. He says I have remarkably high cheekbones. I replay in my head all the wonderful things he has said about me. I can't remember all of them, there have been so many. I try to remember them while I am doing my hair and make-up. I wish I had written some of them down. I used to keep a diary, but I never seem to have time for it, now. Not since Jessica was born.

I wonder when Aubrey will get to meet Jessica. He knows about her, and he often asks how she is getting on at school. I have not told him where I live, or anything about my circumstances, or my real surname, but I have told him my real first name. When we first met, he knew me as Katrina. Now he calls me by my real name. We text each other all the time. He asked me if he could put I-C-E in front of my name in the address book on his mobile phone. I asked him what it meant. He said, 'In Case of Emergency'. He said he had no family, since his mother died, and he never spoke to his ex-wife, and he needed someone who could be contacted if he had an accident. And he asked me. I said yes. In return, I know I can call him up whenever I have a problem that I need to talk through. He is very understanding, and very experienced. He cried once. I texted him to ask if he was free, and he said he was just finishing a meal in a restaurant, but he would ring me when he got back. He did ring me, and I spoke to him about all the problems I had been having with horrible Gary, and the lease, and how behind his men are with the building work he promised to do for me, and the fact that he never leaves me alone when he spends the weekend with me. I told him that Gary (who has appalling teeth) had been quite rough with me, and left me feeling all bruised up there. I don't think he did it maliciously, but it was awful. Aubrey said some very supportive things, and then he started crying. After a minute, he was crying buckets.

'Oh, Rebecca,' he said, 'I worry about you so much.' And then, later on, he sent me a text to say that he was sorry, but he couldn't help it.

I have been thinking recently. Things have been really difficult for some time now. Aubrey has been really sweet about that as well. I couldn't work because I was having quite a heavy period, but it was nearly the day when the direct debit for the mortgage was due to go out, and I was already overdrawn and short by £270. I was talking to Aubrey about it on the phone, and he asked I was free that same evening. I said I was free, but we couldn't do anything because I was on my period. He said it didn't matter. He arrived at the Manchester flat two hours later. He had a new silk tie on, and he had called in at Marks and Spencers and he had brought a bottle of Cava and a little picnic: prawns, coleslaw, crusty bread rolls, stuffed olives and feta cheese, sliced roast beef, potato salad, and two chocolate sundaes. It was lovely. And there was hardly any washing-up. That is the only drawback with the Manchester flat: no dishwasher. He stayed for just one hour that time, after we had finished eating and talking, and then he went home, and he paid me £300. Saved my life. For a month, at least.

Aubrey will be here in about half an hour. Just time for a bit of a tidy-up before he arrives. He is always on time, and he never stays longer than I want him to, though I usually let him stay longer than he has booked for, if I'm free, which I often am nowadays.

*

I have just had the most wonderful text from Aubrey.

> Hello, Rebecca. How are you? I was wondering if you
> wanted to spend a night in Leeds next Friday. I could meet
> you in the station concourse, and then we could have
> dinner and stay in a hotel. I will book dinner and a room at
> 42, The Calls if you are free. Regards, Aubrey. XXXX

I text him back straight away.

> Nice to hear from you Aubrey darling and yes of course I
> am free next Friday, 42 the calls sounds lovely, I've never
> been there but I've looked at it on the internet and it looks
> divine. Can't wait to see you again darling, see you 7.30 at
> leeds station?? xXXXx

That is something to look forward to.

I have been doing some more serious thinking, about the work situation, and about all the things that Aubrey has said to me, and I think it all points to one thing. I am going to tell him that I am stopping work. I am going to ask him if he wants us to go into business together. I have been looking at houses in the country in the South of France. (Aubrey speaks French, I think.) I think we could open a bar or a brasserie or something. And maybe I could carry on working for a bit if we are short of money while the business gets going. I have never had a French client before, except once. At least, I think he had a French accent. He smelt funny, like some kind of yucky, scented hair-oil.

I think I have found a place that we could put in an offer for. Or Aubrey could make an offer for. It is a converted barn in the

31

Dordogne. It is near a village called Belves. It has four bedrooms, three reception rooms, a kitchen, two bathrooms, a stable, and ten acres of land, most of which is currently given over to vineyards. I think Aubrey should be able to afford it. I could sell my house, and he could sell his house, and maybe we would need a mortgage, but I am sure we could afford it. Maybe we might have enough left over to buy some horses to go in the stable. I wonder if there is somewhere that Jessica could go to school. Otherwise, we would have to send her to boarding school in England. Aubrey explained to me once the differences between the French and British education systems, but I wasn't really listening.

*

I have just spotted Aubrey standing on the other side of the barrier in the station. He is on time, of course. He embraces me, and I lean in to kiss him the way I know he likes, but he seems reluctant. The station concourse is a bit too public for Aubrey. He can be shy sometimes. I am sure it is not that he is afraid someone he knows might see us. I am sure it is just people in general.

'The restaurant is not that far, but we'll take a taxi, I think,' he says. I think he is considering my five-inch heels.

42 The Calls turns out to be a classy place. Aubrey remembers that I don't drink red wine, and so he orders a bottle of white: something called Mersault. I would prefer something sparkling, but it should be fine as long as it is not too dry. The waiter pours the wine into a decanter, which he puts on a kind of metal stand some way from the table. He fills our glasses, and refills them from time to time. I think he looked a bit disapprovingly at us once, because he thought we were drinking too quickly. Aubrey did seem to have something on his mind.

'Is this wine OK for you?'

'It's lovely, darling.' It was funny, actually. It tasted like Parma violets. There was a long pause.

'Do you have any other clients like me, er…, Katrina?' I asked him not to call me Rebecca in company unless he hears me refer to myself as Rebecca first. He usually remembers.

'Of course not, darling. There's only one Mister Aubrey.'

'I mean, do you have any other clients that you have the same sort of relationship with as me? Is there anyone else who buys you presents and who you talk to on the phone and ask advice from?'

32

'There is one.' I was thinking about a chap called Simon. He is very nice, and he can be useful sometimes (he's a tax advisor) but I would never think of settling down with him. And I would never tell him about the problems with Gary. I don't think he would understand. He would just tell me to stop seeing him, but of course I can't until I can sort out my finances – or someone helps me to sort them out. I do wish I knew how much Aubrey earns. He hardly ever talks about his job. I think he is something in IT. And I think he got quite a lot of money when his mother died, but I don't know how much of that he lost when he got divorced.

I stopped thinking about money when I realised that neither of us had uttered a word for minutes on end.

'Rebecca, there is something I need to tell you,' he eventually said. He gulped a big mouthful of Mersault, and frowned. He looked very serious. 'I have met someone, and I intend to be faithful to her. I'll have to leave when we have finished dinner. You have the option of going back home in a car I have arranged for you, or you can stay in the hotel room and make your own way back in the morning. I can't see you anymore.' He bows his head and exhales loudly when he has finished speaking. He is gripping the edge of the table with both hands.

I feel sad now. Maybe I'll have to sell the diamond studs after all.

Thomas's Favour

Thomas decided he would allow himself one last reading. He took the shoe box off the top of the bookcase, poured himself a glass of sherry, and took out the first one. He still had all the envelopes. Each one had been carefully slit open with a knife. He sniffed the vellum of the first envelope: there was no perfume, other than the smell of the paper itself, and something indefinable that would always remind him of love, warmth, belonging, and nights of fulfilment.

"My Dearest, Most Beloved Thomas," he read and re-read. Even those words were enough to transport him back to the beautiful, orderly, tasteful and luxurious flat in South Kensington where they had first met, first dined together, first seen each other naked, and first slept together. Thomas had been working part-time as an assistant curator at a private art gallery, and helping out in a barber's shop. He had been short of money: always short of money. No money for clothes; no money for theatre or ballet tickets; no money for taxis - not enough money for a bottle of wine, sometimes. Hilary had fixed that problem: they shared a box at Covent Garden. Hilary had a chauffeur. Hilary's cellar was stocked to bursting with interesting clarets and ports. Hilary had a personal shopper. Hilary had been very generous.

What had Thomas given Hilary in return? He reflected on this as he read further, and got to one of the first passages which contained explicitly sexual references. Some of the letters were, he had to admit, little more than a fairly educated and literary form of pornography. That was one of the things that was so wonderful about them: one of the reasons why he enjoyed reading them so much. They were a diary of the best, most exciting, most unlikely, most exhilarating chapter of Thomas's life. There would never be another Hilary in his life.

The one thing that had made the ending bearable was that Thomas had disciplined himself from the outset to think that it could not and would not last. He was grateful to himself now for having done that. He had actually sat in front of the dressing-table mirror every morning and said, out loud, "You know this is not going to last, don't you?" And he had studied his own face, forcing himself to look at himself as if he were a different person. "DON'T YOU?" he had shouted. And then he had nodded. "Yes, I understand. I understand it cannot last." And then he had finished getting dressed, and gone out to meet Hilary at whichever expensive restaurant or bar or other wonderful place of culture or relaxation they had chosen together, and he had enjoyed every minute of their time together. He could remember every room, every course of every meal, every scene of every play, every sauna, every swim, every walk. These memories were his insurance, his pension, his deposit account. He would keep them safe. He would take them out on cold winter evenings and relive them. They would stop him from getting miserable. They would stop him from growing old before his time.

Thomas made his mind go blank and, while he thought of nothing at all, he fed the letters rapidly through the shredder. He put the paper strips into a brown-paper shopping bag and went out into the yard at the back of his ground-floor flat. He squirted some lighter-fuel over the bag, and set a lighted match to it. It burnt like tinder. A few tiny fragments of ash and paper flew up into the night sky, in mimicry of the ecstasy of Thomas's grief for his beloved lost possessions, but nothing that signified anything. He had made his promise, and he had kept it.

Thomas sat down with his glass of sherry and forced himself to open the first of the contact magazines he had bought that afternoon. He tried to read to the end of the first advertisement, but he could not do it.

He switched on the television. It was Hilary, on "Newsnight". He was outlining how the new government would fight crime while also reducing the prison population. Thomas loved it when Hilary talked his nonsense: it turned him on.

Slow Dance With a Skeleton

I have just finished compiling my ad for the personal column in *Private Eye*. It reads like this.

Renaissance man, 27, 5' 10", clean-shaven, financially solvent, seeks Renaissance woman. Good body (any size) desirable. Good intellect essential. Non-smoker preferred. No Christians.

Private Eye has the most expensive personal column of any journal I have come across, but I am persuaded that this is because it gets the best replies. Money is no object at the moment. I am placing this ad with no expectations in mind: I just want to see what will happen. I don't care whether the consequences are good or bad, as long as they are interesting and unusual.

The ad contains one tiny element of misrepresentation: I am not twenty-seven yet: I am twenty-six (my birthday is in a few weeks). The world has no use for young, single, straight men – certainly not in peacetime.

The ad was published last week, and I have had one reply so far, from a twenty-three year-old woman in Liverpool, called April. She sounds intelligent and educated, but I hope she is more interesting in person than she conveys in her letter. She likes early music and detective stories. I am now in the executive lounge at York railway station, waiting for a train to Liverpool Lime Street that leaves in two hours. The first class carriage on the trans-Pennine train is tiny and definitely not worth the extra expense, but I can easily afford it.

It is eleven a.m. and I am drinking free tea and coffee while I try to do the *Times* crossword. In between bursts of concentration, I am looking around at my fellow travellers, of whom I am delighted to say there are not many. There are a couple of businessmen who were having an irritatingly loud conversation about prospects in Kuwait, but this fortunately ended when one of them had to get up to catch his train. There is an elderly, genteel-looking couple, and a very striking-looking woman who is reading a magazine and sitting on her own. She looks about six feet tall, and has bright red hair and very white skin.

36

Her hair has been forced somehow through a kind of black cylinder, which looks as if it might be made of ebony. The plume of hair sticks up at the back of her head like the flare from a bright red firework. She is wearing what I would call 'goth boots', which are heavy, leather, platform-soled, and decorated with metal plates. Her dress is black, and mostly concealed under her midnight-purple, leather overcoat. She wears an assortment of metal rings in her ears and on her fingers. She is looking with a mixture of sarcastic amusement and harsh disapproval at whatever she is reading. Every so often, she emits a loud guffaw and takes a sip from the cup of black coffee which I noticed earlier she laced with something from a stainless steel flask she keeps in her capacious shoulder-bag.

I get up, ostensibly to refill my cup from the machine at the back of the room, and I deliberately choose my route to enable me to glance down at what the red-haired woman is reading. It is *Private Eye*, and I am almost certain she had turned to the small ads pages. I am trying to think of something to say to her, but my mind is a complete blank.

Back in my seat, I start to wonder whether she has noticed me. She has definitely noticed me now, because she is holding up the hip-flask in plain view and she mouths the words, 'Want some?' She looks at me with an expression that is quizzical and challenging rather than welcoming. I pick up my cup and my belongings, and go and sit in the chair next to hers.

She holds the neck of the flask poised above my cup, which is less than half full.

'Yes, please,' I say, without a moment's hesitation. She obliges with a generous slug which produces coffee flavoured vodka rather than vodka-flavoured coffee. I sip it, and am pleasantly surprised by the smoothness of the mixture. I take two more sips. I take a mouthful. It goes down easily. I take another mouthful. I drain the cup. I want some more. She holds the open flask upside down and shakes it gently from side-to-side in a gesture of defeat.

'Shall I get some more?' I ask her. She looks at me with disdain.

'Do you mean the stuff from the mini-mart in the station? Mm – yummy! It'd be better than meths, I suppose.'

'Back in a few minutes,' I tell her as I get up.

I walk out of the main exit from the station and, there being no queue at the rank, I get straight into the first taxi. I take a short ride to

'Oddbins', buy a bottle of 'Bison Grass' Polish vodka, and return within fifteen minutes. I have the crumpled receipt in my pocket but, without looking at it, I have no idea how much the bottle of vodka cost.

'I was just beginning to get worried,' she calmly informs me as I sit down again in the same chair as before. In spite of herself, her face lights up for a moment as I produce the bottle. She refills her hip-flask, without spilling a drop. We discreetly keep the bottle in its bag, and have another round of stiff vodka-coffees.

'What's your name?' she asks. I don't respond immediately. 'Is that a difficult question?' she continues.

'Harold.'

'Harold?' She sniggers. She throws her head back, closes her eyes, and laughs silently but almost uncontrollably. When she recovers herself, she is almost out of breath. 'You don't look like a "Harold",' she explains, as if that makes everything all right.

'What would you say a "Harold" looks like? Do you want me to stick an arrow in my eye?'

'Good one!' We chink our cups together in a moment of harmonious celebration. She gives me a sidelong glance, and studies me for a moment. I am expecting her to say something, but nothing happens. She returns to her magazine. There being nothing better to do, I go back to my crossword and pour another shot of vodka into my cup.

'Ha!' she exclaims. 'Look at this sad boy.' She reads from the advertisement on the page in front of her.

'Just what the world needs: another twenty-something single man. Cambridge-educated, sensitive, inexperienced, based in West London. Seeks interesting and understanding woman for serious relationship with a view to marriage.'

'He sounds all right,' I protested. And then I thought, 'Why am I advocating on behalf of another, straight, male advertiser?'

'He sounds like a little lost boy who's going to come to a bad end,' she insists. 'And look at this pretentious twat.' She reads my carefully-composed effort, in its entirety. 'Why is it so vitally important that he's clean-shaven?' she asks.

'A lot of women don't like beards.' She looks blank.

'And why does he say he's financially solvent?'

'Wouldn't you object to a partner who is saddled with debt?'

'Would you?'

'I think I would, yes.'

'Why are you seemingly so interested in me, then?'

'Are you telling me that you are saddled with debt?'

She pauses before replying.

'No comment.' Another pause. 'That's you, isn't it?'

'What?'

'That advertisement – you placed it, didn't you?'

'Yes.' She laughs again, more uproariously than before. 'I'm six feet tall, and twenty-eight years old. I could *never* have anything to do with a man who was either shorter or younger than me.'

An hour later, I am on the phone to April, giving her an excuse about a fictitious grandmother who has been suddenly taken ill. I am not going to Liverpool any more: I have been back to the ticket office and am now going to Edinburgh with a tall red-headed goth whose name I still don't know.

*

Her name, as far as I know, is "Cassandra". That is what she told me. She told me a lot of other things. What I mean is that a lot of other things came out of her mouth. Whether "she" was saying them is something that I don't understand.

This is our third night in *The Scotsman* hotel in Edinburgh. Everything is being charged to one of my credit cards. I honestly cannot tell you at this point whether the limit on the card has been blown or not.

I am sitting on the floor in the bathroom with a bottle of whisky, my notebook and a pen. I am writing down what has happened. Don't ask me why I am writing it down. I just don't know what else to do. I probably should be doing something, but I don't know what.

Cassandra is having the latest in a series of what I would call "psychotic episodes". Our first night here was blissful. The second night was weird, verging on scary. All I will say about today is that, the moment Cassandra is physically capable of getting the lift down to the lobby, we are leaving. I hardly slept, but discovered this morning that she had doodled and coloured and written random words and phrases all over the bedside telephone with a biro. One of the things she put was 'Please help me'.

Cassandra started telling me about her life story and previous relationships. To begin with, it was conversational, pleasant, and interesting. We had drinks in the bar. We had dinner. We had another drink after dinner. We moved upstairs, by which point Cassandra had begun to attract attention because of her outbursts and her behaviour. I did not actually push her into the lift, but I certainly wanted to.

This is what Cassandra said, as closely as I can remember.

'I had a boyfriend called Simon. He was the only man I have ever loved. He was gentle and kind and very sensitive. We used to take drugs together. All I ever took was cannabis and speed, but Simon did other things. Our dealer was another goth called Hilary. I always made fun of him because he had a girl's name. He hates me. I tried to get Simon to hold back on what he was taking, but I failed. Hilary sold him something which killed him. I will never forgive Hilary for that, and I will never forgive myself, either. I threatened to tell the police. Ever since, Hilary has been trying to destroy me. He has keys to my house which I think he took off Simon's body when he was dead. He and his crew let themselves in, and they do things like erasing files on my computer, listening to my answerphone, even cooking and leaving the kitchen in a mess – anything to ram it down my throat that my living space is not my own. He also takes my bank card and draws money out of my account. I am about a thousand pounds overdrawn at the moment because of his stealing from me. Hilary got his girlfriend to impersonate me, and they took out a personal loan in my name.'

Don't ask me why she did not get the locks changed, or talk to the bank about the fraudulent transactions, or to the police about the drug-dealing. Don't ask me why she does not seek treatment for her mental illness.

*

I cannot remember how we got back to Cassandra's house.

We had a passably content few weeks, spent mostly in Cassandra's house, which is a rented Victorian terrace. She then started to go down again, and has now been sitting almost unmoving for three days with the curtains closed. Her house is untidy, cluttered and smells of stale incense. She has many prints on the walls: Dali, Bosch, Klimt, Edward Hopper. She has four cats, whom I have had to look after

40

while she has been ill. I hate animals but I felt sorry for them. She has shelves full of books and vinyl records, most of which have been thoroughly clawed by the cats.

I have cleared the ornaments, brass incense-burners, candlesticks, boxes full of spent matches, jewellery cases, vases of dead flowers, records with no covers, books, and cat hairs off the table, and I have written a letter to Cassandra.

My Dearest Cassandra,

You are the most beautiful, captivating, intelligent, fascinating woman I have ever met, or ever expect to meet — when you are rational and not depressed. Unfortunately, I now realise that that is not enough to sustain us.

I cannot live the way you do. If the house were to catch fire, I would call the fire brigade and then get on with the rest of my life. You wouldn't. You say that all I do is call the fire brigade because it's not my house and I don't understand what a fire is like. While we argue, the house burns down. Have you noticed how, after one of our rows has been going on for hours, we move off the original subject and instead have an argument about the argument itself? You say you have a lot of problems, which is true. What you do not say is that most of your problems are capable of solution — some of them by fairly simple means.

The thing I cannot stand about you is the way you allow yourself to be tormented by Hilary. Since you let slip where he lived, every day I have considered going round to his house with an iron bar. You have messed with my sense of justice, you have taken my money, and you have started to erode my sanity. I am now going to walk to York station, and get on a train. That train will take me to the next episode in my life, but you won't be on it.

Love, Harold.

I left the letter on the table, picked up my bag, let myself out quietly, and walked to the station. I was sitting on a bench on the platform, when my phone rang.

I went back to Cassandra's house. Eleven years later, after our divorce, I finally caught the train.

The Toy Fire Engine

Tom Prendergast leaves the office where he is the manager of a team of IT customer support workers. He is known for the tenacity with which he adheres to the letter of service contracts, and he only allows his operators to provide precisely what the customer has paid for. He is going to the Leeds Library, a private subscription library, two years to the day since his only previous visit there, when he had accidentally left his coat behind. He is going to collect the coat. Until he received the letter from the librarian, he had been convinced that he had left the coat in the office where he works, and that it had been stolen by one of the cleaners. Both the cleaners in Tom Prendergast's office are black. It is a good coat, waterproof, from Marks & Spencer. Tom is glad it is being returned.

He walks along the busy street, and occupies a few seconds in trying to avoid the insanely cheerful and talkative woman in magenta overalls with a clipboard, on the back of which is the logo of a charity which runs schemes in the developing world. Tom does not realise that these seconds are wasted: the woman was not intending to try to talk to him.

Outside the door of the library, Tom takes out the swipe card and runs it through the reader. The light flashes red. Tom curses, and blames the grey-haired, doddering, speck-eyed gits who run the library for the machine's failure to read the card and open the door first time. He tries the card again. The light flashes green. Tom takes nothing back.

Inside, he notices the stairlift which is a modern addition to the stone and wrought iron staircase. Tom realises that this is a necessary addition because so many of the members are old codgers and spastics. He is unaffected by the way in which the utilitarian stairlift clashes with the elegant patterns in the Georgian ironwork. He ascends on his own two feet to the door of the main reading room. Ignoring the notice board, and all the messages displayed around the entrance, he goes through. The bespectacled female member of the library staff greets him cheerfully, recognises him, and instantly recalls that Tom is here to collect his coat. She also knows that he has never borrowed a book. His last visit was to return some books that had been borrowed by his father, a long-time member of the library who had died and bequeathed his membership to Tom. She presses a button on the intercom to summon the Chief Librarian who she surmises will want to talk to Mr Prendergast about his overdue subscription.

'I'm here to collect my coat.'

'Of course, Mr Prendergast.' The librarian turns to her colleague, who has been sitting behind the counter, reading a magazine. 'Jackie, will you just pop into Katy's office and get Mr Prendergast's coat, please? It's a black one with concealed buttons and a collar.' Jackie smiles and raises the folding section of the counter so that she can perform the errand. They hear laboured footsteps descending the spiral staircase. It is Mr Bennett, the Chief Librarian. They hear a child's cry. It is Oscar, Mr Bennett's four-year-old grandson, who is playing with a toy fire engine on the floor of the gallery at the top of the stairs, watched over by his mother, who is Mr Bennett's daughter-in-law. The rules say that children under 11 years of age are not allowed in the library, but everybody likes Oscar and no objection to his visits has ever been registered. Oscar loves to look at pictures in books, particularly ones with a great deal of red in them, and is a better reader than most children his age. Tom is irritated by Oscar's burbling commentary on the fire engine, and by Mr Bennett's descent, which is slowed by his arthritic knees. The young, smiling Jackie has to stand at the foot of the staircase and wait for it to be clear for her to ascend. Tom thinks about the fact that Mr Bennett could have waited to allow Jackie up first. He is so angry at Mr Bennett's stupid selfishness at blocking the stairs with his shuffling, disabled body that he begins to want to kill him.

Mr Bennett arrives painfully at the desk next to Tom. A woman with a ridiculous orange jacket; over-stuffed green, vinyl handbag; lesbian shoes, and bird's nest hair comes in and wants to approach the counter, and so Mr Bennett walks painfully away again, to a spot next to a huge card index in wooden drawers, under the gallery. Tom follows him, and narrowly succeeds in suppressing the urge to push him in the back to make him move faster.

'I wanted to talk to you about your subscription.'

'What subscription?'

'We like to have as many members as possible on direct debit.'

'Direct debit for what? What are you talking about?'

'It's eighty pounds a year. Your dad used to pay by direct debit. We were all very sad when he departed.'

At that moment, Jackie arrives with Tom's coat. Tom wants to grab the coat and run out of the door, away from these mad people with their annoying, irrelevant, money-scrounging questions. 'Oh, the coat,' announces Mr Bennett, fatuously. Jackie smiles and hands the coat to Tom, who immediately starts to put it on over the jacket of his Marks & Spencer suit. 'Would you like to know how we knew it was yours?'

Tom is about to snarl the word 'No' at Mr Bennett, when Oscar propels the toy fire engine as hard as he can towards the railings of the gallery. Oscar's mother stamps her foot down on the parquet floor, but just too late to prevent the model, cast in metal, from bouncing off one of the railings and over the edge. The fire engine lands on the crown of Tom's head. The impact sets off a complex neurological episode but does not break the skin, nor apparently cause Tom any discomfort. Jackie and Mr Bennett cannot tell whether the toy fire engine hit Tom or not. They think it probably did, but cannot understand why he is not complaining about it.

'Yes, I do,' Tom assures Mr Bennett. 'I most certainly do. Please tell me all about it.'

Mr Bennett extends a hand towards one of the outside pockets of the coat which Tom is now wearing. He pauses for a moment, as if to say, 'May I?' and then pulls out a glossy envelope with the name of an expensive jeweller on it.

'We found this receipt inside. It has your name and address on it.' Mr Bennett hands the envelope to Tom, who opens it and stares at the receipt. It is a document that he had completely forgotten about until this moment. It is a receipt for a platinum and diamond ring that he bought four years previously for a woman who went by the name of Bernice, and who worked from a rented apartment in a converted warehouse by the river in the centre of Leeds.

Tom receives a flood of recollections about Bernice. He remembers the first time he tried to ring her on his mobile phone. He had been in a place where the signal was poor and he kept getting cut off. They had communicated by text message instead, sending many messages to each other, some of them not strictly relevant to the transaction they were dealing with. He had arranged to see Bernice the following Friday lunchtime. He had been excited to see her. She had been the most beautiful woman he had ever seen. He had loved talking to Bernice about every subject they could think of. He had been surprised by how interested she had been to hear about other women he had had relationships or encounters with. He had been surprised by how enthusiastic Bernice seemed to be when they had sex, and by how deeply he had fallen in love with her. He had been surprised when, one day when they had spent several hours together, Bernice had told him that he should stop calling her Bernice and instead call her Kirsty. He had asked why she wanted to be called Kirsty, and she had said that she wanted to be called Kirsty because that was her real name, and then they had both cried, with sadness at first but then with happiness. He had loved her so much that he had told her that he did not have enough money to keep coming to see her, and that he wanted her to get a normal job so that they could get married. He remembers how much he had wanted to marry Kirsty and have children with her. He had wanted a little boy first, like Oscar – exactly like Oscar. Tom has only seen Oscar through the railings of the gallery but he can still tell that Oscar is a beautiful boy. He remembers that he had been so much in love with Kirsty that he had not even been angry with her when she had told him that she would not see him any more after he had asked her to marry him. He remembers how he had not even been angry with her when she kept the ring he had bought, the receipt for which he is holding in his hand. He tucks the envelope with the receipt back inside his pocket. He is glad he kept it. He remembers why he kept it. He regrets not having looked at it more often in the time before he mislaid the coat.

Tom picks the toy fire engine up off the floor. As he does so, he notices that one of the small plastic ladders which clip onto the top has come off, and landed a few feet away just under the card index drawers. Tom gets down on his hands and knees and reaches for the tiny ladder. He carefully fits the ladder back into the little grooves which hold it in place. He walks up the spiral staircase to the gallery, places the fire engine on the floor in front of where Oscar is sitting, and walks back down again to resume his conversation with Mr Bennett. He is still thinking about Kirsty, and has tears in his eyes. Mr Bennett thinks Tom must have a pain in his head, but he does not dare to ask after Tom's welfare because he is worried that Mr Prendergast might threaten to take out a personal injury claim against the library, which would mean financial ruin unless they could claim for it on the insurance policy.

'About the subscription,' continues Mr Bennett. Tom notices that Jackie has returned to her seat behind the desk, and has resumed reading her magazine. Tom hopes that the article Jackie is reading is interesting and educational. Tom hopes that Jackie is studying something that is going to make her an even better librarian, and boost her career prospects.

'Yes, of course. The subscription. How much is it? You said it was eighty pounds a year.'

'That's right.'

'How many years do I owe?'

'Three years, including the coming year. We prefer our members...'

'To pay by direct debit. Of course. Have you got the payment details?' Mr Bennett picks up a form from a set which are on display on a table in front of the card index drawers. Tom looks at the form and sees that it has on it the sort code and account number for the library's bank account.

'Is it OK to use a mobile phone in here?' he asks.

'You can't take a call in here, but you can read texts or do anything that doesn't make too much noise. Minimal noise is allowed in here. The other reading rooms are silent.'

'I just want to access my bank account. I'll go outside.'

'No, it's OK...'

'I'll go outside.'

Tom walks out of the door to the top of the stairs. He notices that the chair of the stair lift has moved from the bottom to the top, from which he infers that the learned-looking lady in the orange jacket who came in earlier must have a mobility problem. The thought that two of the people he has met today have had a mobility problem makes him cry gently while he is working the banking app on his phone. He sets up a payment to the library's account for two hundred and forty pounds, and goes back inside.

'When can I start to read the books?'

'You can start right away,' says Mr Bennett.

'Thank you,' says Tom. Mr Bennett slowly goes back to his office, up the spiral staircase.

Tom looks around the main reading room. Behind the desk, there are shelves full of books. In the centre of the room are parallel shelves with books loaded onto them from both sides. All around the walls of the room are shelves which reach up so high that you would need a ladder to reach the topmost ones. Tom notices that there is indeed a ladder for this purpose. It has a sign on it which says, "For Staff Use Only". Tom fervently hopes that the ladder is safe. He looks up at the shelves which line the gallery above him. He looks through the entrances to two other reading rooms, all lined with books. He wants to read and absorb every single one of them. Some of them look ancient, older even than the Georgian building he is standing in. Some of them are huge: so large that it would require two people to lift one of them.

Tom staggers round the main reading room, and in and out of what he doesn't know are called the Art Reading Room and the New Room. He feels drunk. In the Art Reading room he picks a book off the shelf at random. It is called 'Waterhouse'. He opens it at a random page. It is a beautiful picture of a lady. She has long, dark hair. She is leaning forward, partly in the direction of the viewer and partly to one side. She seems to be looking at something which the viewer cannot see. She is wearing a pale coloured dress. She has something in her hand, which looks to Tom like something to do with sewing or weaving. He scans down the picture and notices that just underneath a patch of gold embroidery on the lady's dress is what looks like a repeated elliptical doodle done with a blue pen, as if by a child. Tom cannot help imagining Oscar, blue biro in hand, unaccountably allowed to be in front of this old and valuable painting, squiggling on it, as high up as he can reach, round and round and round and round, until his mother comes to pick him up and move him away. Tom thinks of Oscar's mother gently scolding him, and then finding him something less easily damaged but still interesting to look at. He thinks how wonderful it would be if the painting were not greatly impaired by the childish action, and if nobody really minded anyway, because to get upset and shout about it would not be worth a child's tears. Tom puts the book back on the shelf, and wanders into the next reading room, at the back of the library.

A black sign with white lettering on it displays the word "ARCHITECTURE" above the next bookcase that confronts Tom.

Every shelf is crammed. The air in this room smells of dust and slowly-decaying manuscripts. Most of these books look old. Their spines are olive green, or bronze-coloured, with black or gold lettering. Right in front of Tom's face is a book which is obviously new. It is a paperback. He picks it from the shelf. It is about the architecture of Leeds. He opens it at a randomly-chosen page. He sees a set of photographs of a building called 'The Mansion', which overlooks Roundhay Park. One of the photographs shows the lush green of the park which slopes down in front of The Mansion, down to a place where there is a funfair. Tom can just pick out the roundabout which he remembers from his childhood. It was the only ride or amusement that Tom wanted to have a go on. His dad would give him some money for rides and sweets, and he would spend every penny of it on the roundabout and, when all his money was spent, he wanted to go home. Sometimes, his dad would give him a bit more money for another couple of rides.

Tom goes back into the main reading room, still holding the book which has a label on its cover which says, "FOR REFERENCE ONLY: NOT TO BE REMOVED FROM THE NEW ROOM." He looks and listens to see if Oscar is still there. He is, but he and his mother have come down the stairs and are in front of the counter. Oscar's mother is trying to put his coat on him, which is not made any easier by Oscar's persistence in holding onto his toy fire engine. Tom puts the book in his pocket.

'Please can I hold your fire engine for a minute?'

'Oh, I wish you would,' says Oscar's mother, thinking that Tom has intervened to help her get the coat on. Oscar considers the question, and cautiously offers the fire engine to Tom, who reverently accepts it.

Tom holds the toy fire engine in both hands, and peers more and more closely at it. He looks into the cab, where the firemen are sitting. There are three rows of seats: two at the back for the fire crew, and one at the front for the driver and one other fireman. Tom's gaze narrows onto the driver. That is where he used to sit, when he was a child, on the roundabout: in the driver's seat of the fire engine. There was a hinged door which opened and closed, which you kept shut by turning a little chrome handle. The outside was glossy red and the inside was pale blue. There was a big brass steering wheel which went round and round. The steering wheel was always cold when Tom first touched it, but he never minded that. All he wanted was for the roundabout to keep going round, and for him to be able to pretend that he was steering the fire engine, and for his dad to give him a few more coins for another ride when the man in the denim jacket at the centre of the roundabout made it stop so that the other children could get off. He is there again, on a day in early summer in Roundhay Park. He can smell the damp air under the trees, and see the patches of sunlight and the colours of the rides, and hear the noise of the fair and the other children. He can see his dad waving to him and tapping his watch to tell him it will be time to go home for tea soon. Tom realises that sitting in the driver's seat of the fire engine on the roundabout was, until this moment, the only time in his life he was happy. He also realises that his dad tried to give him many other things in life besides a few more coins for another go on the roundabout, but Tom could always think of a reason why he did not want them, though he cannot now remember what those reasons were.

Tom looks away from the toy fire engine for an instant, and thinks that it might be a good thing if he donated some of his savings to this library, which he can tell is in need of financial support, so that people like Oscar will be able to go on enjoying it.

Oscar and his mother are ready to leave now. Tom bends down to hand the toy fire engine back to Oscar. He straightens. He reaches into his pocket, the one where he put the book on architecture, for his mobile phone, with the intention of transferring some money from his savings account to donate to the library, feels funny, and dies.

49

Frozen Veg

I have been working from home today, and I am now looking at my watch every two minutes to see how long it will be before Gemma gets home. The decision I have to make is whether I start drinking before or after she arrives. Jacob has gone to his dad's. His dad picked him up a few minutes ago. He was 7 minutes early, for the first time ever.

I have been on the phone for most of the day. There were some vitally important emails I needed to read before a telephone conference this afternoon, but my stupid laptop crashed. I spent two hours talking to the PC support desk, and then another twenty minutes trying to get through to someone in the office who could log in to my account and forward the messages to my home email address. The company has a secure email system that can tell the difference between a company PC and any other, which was why I had to track somebody down who was in the office. I don't know why I work in the IT industry: I hate computers. I should have had a new laptop three years ago. The client asked me a load of stupid questions on the conference call. It was a waste of time, as usual, but I had to show them that I had read all the documents and retained the important details. It might have been easier to stand if Jacob had not been watching the same episode of the same programme on the Disney Channel for the twentieth time. I couldn't work out why the TV was so loud, even by Jacob's standards. When I went in there to tell him to turn it down, I found out why: he was sitting there with his headphones on, listening to his iPod. He said that he needed it that loud so that he could hear the TV over the sound of the iPod. I asked him politely if it might not be a good idea to decide between the TV or the iPod, but he just said no. It was like that all day until his dad came for him. His dad and Gemma both hit him if he misbehaves, but I am not allowed to – not that I would want to, anyway.

Gemma's parking the car now. She collapses through the door, carrying two bags full of case files. She must have been to see the Hendersons today. I can see it in her face. Two parents, unmarried, like we are, unable to cope with the burden of looking after their children. Unlike us, they are unemployed. Unlike us, they have four children rather than one. Unlike us, the father is also the biological father, of all four children. Unlike us, everything they get wrong about parenting now comes to the attention of local government. Gemma has picked up a habit of going round and remarking on the things that the Hendersons have been reported for which are also wrong in our house. These are mainly to do with untidiness, dirt, lack of exercise and mental stimulation for Jacob, and poor diet.

I have another set of decisions to make: I can pretend to listen to Gemma talking about her visit to the Hendersons, and offer sympathy, or I can try to signal to her that I have had a stressful day and don't want to hear about it, or I can really listen to her talking about the Hendersons and get emotionally involved. To do the last thing I need alcohol.

It is not yet six o'clock. Gemma opens the litre bottle of Smirnoff I bought at the weekend, ostensibly for her, and because it was on special offer. She adds diet cola but no ice to a stiff measure and reclines on the sofa in front of the television. I hate the programme she is watching, but I am grateful for the issuance of permission to start drinking. The litre bottle of vodka is my reserve for later. Gemma will probably drink about a quarter of it and then go to bed. The only other alcohol we have in the house is a can of strong Belgian lager, left over from the weekend. I want more beer, and I want wine. I need permission to go to the shops.

'What do you want for dinner?' I ask.

'Do you mean, "tea"?'

'No. Dinner.'

'Tea.'

'Dinner.'

'Tea.'

'Dinner.'

'Well, for TEA, I don't know what I would like.'

'Steak?'

'Yes, possibly steak. Have we got any steak?'

'We have some very nice sirloin steak, but nothing to have it with. Shall I go to the shops?'

'Do you need to go to the shops?'

'We haven't got anything to go with the steak, and so I was going to go to the shops to buy some spinach, or some broccoli.'

51

'Do we need spinach or broccoli?'

'Yes, we do, unless you want steak on its own.'

'Haven't we got anything in the freezer?'

'Shall I have a look?'

'Yes, you have a look.' I take an empty plastic beaker out of the cupboard.

We have two freezers. One in the kitchen and one in the utility room. While I am looking in the one in the utility room, I take the can of Belgian lager from the fridge. I put my finger on the ring-pull, and crack it at the same moment as pulling out the freezer-drawer which is always frozen in place and makes a loud noise as you draw it out. I hold the beaker nearly horizontally and pour the can into it. I push the drawer back and close the freezer and take a long draught of my secluded beer. The beer is strong and was bought partly for its cheapness. It has a strong flavour and tastes partly of alcohol. I drink a quarter of it before coming out of the utility room and into the kitchen where Gemma can see me.

'I think we need some more things to go with the steak.'

'Where are you thinking of going?'

'The Co-op.'

'The Co-op?'

'Yes. The Co-op.'

'Why don't you just go to Pollard's?'

'They don't sell fresh veg at Pollard's, other than potatoes – and they are quite often starting to sprout.'

'Yes, but they do sell booze. You were going out to buy booze.'

'Yes, I was going out to buy booze, but I was going out to buy something to go with the steak as well.'

'It's Tuesday.'

'Yes, that is undoubtedly a fact: it is Tuesday.'

'You're getting drunk every night.'

'No, I'm not.'

'Thursday night, Friday night, Saturday night, Sunday night, and now Tuesday.'

'That wouldn't be every night: you missed out Monday. And I didn't get drunk on Sunday.'

'Only because you were recovering from Saturday.'

'Do you want anything?'

'Like what?'

'I don't know. Anything from the shop.'

'We need diet coke.'

'Anything else?'

'No. I think that is it. You'll be gone for ages.'

'No, I won't.'

'You will. You were gone an hour, last time. I don't want to be on my own for an hour.'

'It was more like half an hour.'

'It was ages.'

'I'll be as quick as I can.'

I go back into the utility room to look in the fridge to see if it prompts me to think of anything we need. While I am checking how much butter we have, I see a quarter bottle of vodka that I had forgotten was still there. I take it out carefully, sliding another bottle along the shelf, away from it, first, to avoid clinking. It has about five measures left in it. I pick up a small towel from the pile of washing in front of the machine, and use it to muffle the sound as I unscrew the cap of the bottle. I drink the vodka down in two gulps, concentrating to make sure I swallow it properly and don't start coughing. I put the cap back on the bottle, using the towel again, and put the empty bottle back where I got it from, on the bottom shelf inside the door of the fridge. I'll dispose of it later, after Gemma has gone to bed. I take another long draught from my lager, partly in the hope that the smell of the lager, which Gemma has seen, will mask the smell of the vodka, which she hasn't. After another big mouthful, I have finished the contents of the beaker. I take two shopping bags out of the cupboard, and go back into the kitchen and put the beaker down by the sink, looking away from the seating area where Gemma is. I put my jacket on, pat myself to make sure I have got my wallet and my phone, and leave the house. As I close the door, I glance down at the recycling box, three-quarters full of crushed beer cans, wine bottles, and spirit bottles. It will be another eight days before it is collected.

I start walking briskly. I don't understand why Gemma thinks that the duration of a single visit to the shops is a long time, but I don't mean to be away longer than necessary. I get to the top of the street, and turn onto the main road. I can feel the alcohol begin to affect me. I walk more slowly. As I pass the entrance to the pedestrian subway, I notice a green beer bottle which has been placed, not thrown, on the pavement. I can see that the bottle is half-full of liquid. I wonder if the liquid is rainwater, or piss, or flat beer. I pass by, and don't investigate.

In the window of Pollard's are small ads, hand-written on cards that have been there for so long that the sun has turned them from white to brown and made them curl at the edges. The area in front of the counter is cramped and cluttered, particularly if the glum-looking woman behind the counter is having a long conversation with one of the locals, which she often is. I ask the customer who has completed her purchases to move, so that I can pick up a basket from the stack wedged between the entrance and the counter. She looks at me with dismay, but I reach behind her and leave it to her to evaluate the risk of the edge of the metal basket catching her as I pull it off the stack.

As I start looking at the shelves, I realise that I have not made a list. I think I must be going mad: I always make a list. I consider going home, but I realise that I would have to reopen the whole argument with Gemma about whether we really need anything, and about alcohol, and so I stay in the shop. I try to remember what it is we need. I might as well start with the booze for me.

Before choosing beer, I touch one of each kind of can to see if any of them have been recently restocked and not had time to get cold. The woman next to the baskets is looking at me. I ignore her. The selection on offer is poor. The only really strong lagers are things that Gemma will recognise, such as Carlsberg Special Brew. There are some strong ciders, but I don't often drink cider and, even though Gemma does drink it, she might take the buying of cider to mean another step on the road to alcoholism. Besides which, Gemma might decide to drink some of it before I do, even though she says it is fattening. I pick four cans of Grolsch, which are nice and cold, five per cent alcohol, and inconspicuous. Now for the wine.

The red wine selection is even worse than the beer. Most of it seems to be from California. Most of it seems to be described as "fruity", which I take to mean that it is red wine for people who don't like red wine. I decide to take a gamble on one from Sicily.

The basket feels heavy as I try to remember what else I have come to buy. All I can remember is booze and that we definitely don't need butter, which I would probably not buy from Pollard's anyway, because it would cost a pound more than it would from a supermarket, and be less fresh. I decide that the only thing to do is to make a circuit of the whole shop, and see if that reminds me of what I have come for. The shelves are untidy and, with the exception of the confectionary display, there does not seem to be much of a system in use. The rack where they keep the non-food items is a mess: rulers and protractors covered in dust are mixed up with sink-plungers, disposable lighters, baking parchment, sticking plaster, and rubber bands which are so old that they have started to go stiff. A few assorted packets look as if they have been opened in order to sell, or steal, a single item. If basket-blocking woman were not still looking at me, I might try to tidy it up.

I look at the sweets, and think of buying a bar of Galaxy cookie crumble for Jacob, but then I remember that he is at his dad's tonight. If I buy a bar and Jacob is not there to consume it immediately, Gemma will probably eat it and then tell me off for having put temptation in her way.

I look at the bread, or what is left of it at this time of day. I nearly always buy bread when I go shopping, because of the constant necessity to avoid having no bread to make Jacob's school lunch in the morning. Again, I remember that he won't be at home in the morning, because he has gone to his dad's. I do a survey of the sell-by dates on the few remaining packets. None has more than three days left on it. A packet of four brown rolls at the back is a day out of date, and has three small spots of green and two of grey mould visible through the cellophane. I put the loaf that has three days left in the basket. I still can't remember what I was supposed to be buying, but I believe that, even if I go round the shop again, and look at even the tinned sweetcorn and the Fray Bentos pies and the 'Camp' coffee and the top-shelf magazines, I won't be able to remember.

I go to the counter, and try to ignore the conversation between the assistant and basket-blocking woman, which is still going on in the same trivial monotone. I put the beer and wine in one shopping bag, and the bread in the other. I have to ask basket-blocking woman to move again, so that I can get to the door. I walk a few yards from the shop, without committing myself to any particular direction.

I look across the main road to the street where the Co-op is. The steak we have is good quality, and merits fresh vegetables to be served with it. I don't mind cooking: I like cooking. I can drink lager while I am cooking, and a more elaborately-prepared meal means time for one more can, before I go onto red wine with the meal and, finally, vodka if Gemma goes to bed early. I also look at the pub, the Halfway House. A pint of real ale would be lovely, just now, and would only take me a little out of my way. I look back the way I came, back towards home.

I remember that we have some green beans and some spinach in the freezer.

I place the shopping on the ground and take out my phone. The battery of the phone is running down, but I have enough charge left to send Gemma a text. *Just finished at Pollard's. Coming home. We can have frozen veg.* Gemma texts back straight away. *Oh good. Can't wait for you to get here my darling. xxx*

Just as I am stepping through the door, I realise that I have forgotten the diet coke. Had I remembered earlier, I might have gone back for it. I look at my watch and realise that Pollard's was almost on the point of closing as I left the shop, and is certainly shut by now.

Gemma is still lying on the sofa with the television on.

'I forgot the diet coke,' I tell her.

'So what did you get?'

'Some booze, and some bread.'

'We didn't need bread. So you got booze for you, bread that we didn't need, and that is it.'

'Yes. I'm sorry. Pollard's is closed now. Do you want me to walk up to the Co-op for some diet coke?'

'You'd be gone another age. What booze did you get?'

'Four cans of lager and a bottle of red wine.'

'I'll have wine then.'

I take the screw-top off the wine, and pour two glasses. I am not going to drink mine yet, but I want to reserve some in case Gemma drinks the rest of the bottle. I pour her a generous measure – about as much as the glass will hold without danger of spillage. She smiles as I hand it to her. I pour myself some lager, and get the steaks out of the fridge. Gemma likes hers well done, and so I'll put it in the pan on its own for a few minutes before I put mine in. I fill a pan with water, ready for the frozen veg.

Not For One Night Only

I'm sorry if I pause a lot when I'm speaking, but I've never been to a therapist before. What I am about to tell you is going to make you think I am insane. Paranoid schizophrenic, or delusional, or something. Anyway, if I'm insane, then Kath is as well, because she saw and heard it all. She bore the brunt of some of it.

My father died before my mother. He was a lot older than she was. They met when he was a lecturer at Leeds College of Commerce, and she was one of his students. You'd get the sack for that sort of behaviour now, but my father told me it was common in the early sixties. My mother had left school at sixteen, with not a clue what she wanted to do in life, other than get away from her mother – who was a fascist. She married my father when she was nineteen, and I was born when she was twenty-one.

When I was about eight years old, she enrolled at university to do a law degree. She turned out to have a talent for the law. Within two years of graduating, she had gone back to the department as a lecturer. Her classes were very popular, because she was passionately interested in what others might regard as very dry subjects, and very good at conveying what the law meant in practice. She also had a dramatic way of talking. Her constant exaggeration and melodrama were hell to live with, but came across very strikingly and memorably in a seminar or tutorial.

Our house, with my venerable father, who also had a legal background, talking like a judge, and my mother like an advocate, took on the tone of a set of chambers, or a courtroom. We could be talking about something perfectly ordinary, like what happened to the last satsuma in the fruit bowl, and the two commonest words in the conversation would be "alleged" and "misrepresentation". It was like living inside a never-ending legal argument. My friends thought my parents were weird, and they often ended up thinking I was weird as well, because I had to use the same magisterial method of communication in order to make myself understood.

My mother left the university after a few years and became a solicitor. She turned out to be even better at that than lecturing. She

57

completed her articles and, within five years of qualifying, she was a full equity partner in a successful firm. A couple of years after I graduated, my mother paid off all my student debts. The money was very welcome, but came with a great long lecture about the value of hard work, and the need for thrift, and how she would never be able to afford to do this again, and so on. By the time she had finished, I was on the point of wanting to throw the cheque back at her. But I kept hold of it, of course.

My mother's circle of business associates and clients and hangers-on grew larger and larger, and she threw more and more extravagant dinner parties, with more and more expensive bottles of wine. It was all a bit hard on my father, who was getting old by then. At first, he went along with it, and then he started to object, which my mother ignored, and then he became too befuddled to really know what was happening. My mother kept wheeling him out at these dinner parties on the strength of his past reputation, but he ended up as a figure of fun by the time he died, which upset me.

A few years before my father died, my mother had had an affair with a man called Peter from the university's anthropology department. Peter's wife had threatened to leave him, and when the affair became known, they both said that they had decided to end it. Peter stopped coming to our house, of course. I must admit that I missed him a bit at the endless dinner parties. When he was around, my mother seemed a bit less silly and melodramatic. Less loud.

When my dad died, I received a legacy of one thousand pounds, and everything else he had owned went to my mother. I was glad when he finally went, because he had lost his mind and was in a lot of discomfort from various illnesses, but I have missed him every day since the time we had our last proper conversation, which was out on the lawn in the back garden, on a summer day. He sat in a deck chair and told me his life story, from birth to the present moment. It took until dusk. He never repeated himself, or got anything out of order. I sometimes wish I had recorded it, or taken notes.

My mother decided to move to the firm's London office. She kept her old house, but only lived in it at the weekend. The rest of the time, she lived in a flat near the City with Peter. Peter had retired (he was only a few years younger than my dad) and loved living rent-free in central London. Things carried on like that, with the house and the flat getting more and more full of all the wine and books and the apparatus for my mother's various fads. She complained about everybody and everything around her, from trains that would not run on time to her Brazilian maid, who she said used too much bleach. One day my mother got so fed up of being short of breath in the flat – so she claimed, because of chlorine fumes – that she sacked the maid. A few weeks later, she went to the doctor, got a referral to see a lung specialist, and was diagnosed with cancer, which she had probably had for years. The maid did not get her job back.

My mother tried to make a dinner party out of her condition. She would invite people round to her private room while she was having chemotherapy in St George's Hospital. They all went on about how brave she was, and how she was going to beat cancer, just like she had beaten every other adverse situation in her life. They kept telling me about how she had been telling jokes while they were pumping her full of medication that burned her veins and would have had a normal person in agony. She invited me to one of these gatherings, but I refused.

The one person who took even longer than my mother to realise what was happening was Peter. He emerged as, by turns, a marshmallow who thought my mother was just ill rather than dying, and then a gold-digger who wanted to get his hands on my mother's estate. He seemed to have no difficulty in switching between these states as frequently as his purposes required.

I remember the day she died. I was present, at the hospice. That morning, Peter had lost his mobile phone. My mother, on intravenous morphine, had been more-or-less awake. She had declared, 'Peter, you are useless'. He laughed, not realising that she had meant it at face value. Those were her last words. She spent the rest of the day in a morphine stupor and then, for no apparent reason, she woke up and looked around her, as if she was alert but didn't recognise where she was. A nurse happened to be in the room at that moment, and she said that they often did that, near the end. The nurse started stroking my mother, which was a brave and compassionate thing to do, because my mother's immune system had long since shut down, and she was undergoing something called "viral blooming", in which the body becomes a living Petri-dish for any pathogen which happens to be passing. If you think that sounds hideous, you should see what it looks like.

I believed the nurse. I believed my mother was about to die. I didn't know what to do. I was sitting by the bed, next to Peter. I knew this was only going to happen once. I reached out, and I held Peter's hand. It didn't feel like it used to feel when I held my dad's hand. I felt foolish, but I had a conviction that it was the right thing to do: that my mother's death should be accompanied by at least a semblance of togetherness and warmth.

My mother did die then, just as the nurse had said she would. I went home, and slept soundly for the first time in a fortnight. The following day, the legal entanglements started.

As well as the intricacies and frustrations of the administration of the estate, and the eye-wateringly high cost of the London lawyers that my mother had engaged to write her will, there was the physical problem of trying to deal with the piles of stuff that my mother had accumulated. The first thing I did was to take a load of paperbacks to a book bank. I had to stop feeding them in, because I had filled it. I took her dresses and hats to the shop run by the hospice where she had died. Peter went mad with me. He wanted everything preserved. I was speechless. I wanted to move on. I wanted to be able to move out from under the shadow that my mother's past life was casting over me. He wanted to do everything possible to deny the fact that my mother had, as he insisted on putting it, "passed away". He wanted everything to stay the same except, of course, the execution of my mother's will, preferably on his terms.

The West End solicitor, while expensive, turned out at least to be reasonably competent. However, the will that my mother had devised, and certain other aspects of her affairs, were grotesque. First of all, Peter was an executor, as well as being one of the principal legatees. That meant that he had to agree to any decision made about the estate.

And then we could not find the deeds to my mother's house. We looked everywhere, including in the safe deposit boxes held by her old firm, where all my mother's papers were reputed to be. We searched the London flat. We searched the house itself. Nothing. The only item of note that turned up was a Laura Ashley carrier bag full of sick-making love letters between my mother and Peter. The postmarks on them showed that they had been exchanged frequently and had not stopped during the period between Peter's wife's threat to leave him and the death of my father. I hardly dared to delve into the bag, but I forced myself to read the top three or four of the cards and letters, and the details showed that the assignations, as well as the correspondence, had continued, without even a pause.

Kath and I were considering selling our own house and moving into my mother's, the house I had grown up in. It was nice and big, and had all kinds of fond associations for me, but it needed a huge amount of work doing on it. Some of the ceilings were so cracked that the neighbour I had asked to check the place over from time to time refused to go into the bedrooms. And junk was everywhere. We counted at least four hundred bottles of wine in the cellar, not including some in unopened cases which we probably missed. Kath, who knew nothing about wine, started googling some of the labels, and found that a few of them were worth two or three hundred pounds a bottle, whereupon she insisted that I stop drinking them. I told her that I was only drinking the ordinary stuff, but she insisted that I might drink something auctionable by accident. The stress was getting to both of us, and we had endless rows.

Peter took to inviting me to his house, once a week at the same time, for a fractious meeting rather than a cup of tea. It was like being summoned by the headmaster. We fell out about the flat in London. He did not want it to be sold. And then, when the solicitor explained to him that it had to be sold, he wanted to buy it for himself. He insisted that all the paperbacks, and the cooking utensils, and the clothes, and the shoes, and the handbags, and the unmatching furniture, and the photographs of places that I had never been to and people I had never known, should all be left exactly where they were, as if in a time capsule, because he wanted to carry on living in it just as he had done before. The solicitor pointed out that it was in the interests of the estate for us to get the best possible price for the flat, and that this would require tidying it up. Peter still moaned.

We shared a taxi after one of the estate meetings at the solicitor's office in Mayfair. Peter said, 'It is all right – we can charge the expense to the estate', which was true, and equivalent to saying, 'to the residuary legatee', which was me.

Peter engaged his own solicitor because he wanted some of the money from my mother's death-in-service insurance. How this was awarded was up to a retired partner from my mother's firm. He decided to award Peter a hundred thousand pounds. I produced a handwritten note, signed and dated, which I had taken during an earlier conversation with my mother in which she had said that she wanted all this money to go to me. The retired partner said that he thought my mother might have changed her mind, because the latest draft of the will showed that the amount she had left Peter had gone from one hundred thousand to two hundred thousand. He ignored the note, and made the grant to Peter from the insurance money as well.

My anger that Peter was interfering in so many aspects of my life turned to clinical depression and I ended up on Prozac. Kath felt so worried about me that we even started to have fewer rows. I got a phobia about crossing the road, because I knew that, until the estate came out of administration, if I got knocked down and killed, everything that had been my mother's would go to Peter.

The administration was eventually ended, by which point I was so exhausted that I could not celebrate it. There was no breaking of tape, no finish line – just a gradual lessening of solicitor's letters and meetings with Peter and learning about details of probate law that previously I had never known existed. The legal trust that had been established by my mother's will was wound up, and I got what was left of the estate, and Kath and I did our best to settle down. At least we had plenty to read and plenty to drink. We even managed to get the old house refurbished, without too much injury to our relationship.

And then I received a letter from my mother. It was postmarked the day before it arrived. It was definitely her handwriting, and it said that she would coming to stay in a few days, and we should make sure the sheets on the spare bed were properly aired.

I thought Peter, or somebody, was trying to play a sick joke on me. I went straight back on Prozac, and tried to work out what was happening. Kath simply refused to believe it. I examined the letter as carefully as I could. It actually felt as if my mother had written it. The paper was a sheet from a batch of headed notepaper that my mother had ordered when I was little, and hardly ever used. It smelt faintly of Calvin Klein's 'Eternity' and cigarette smoke – the odours I always associate with her. It looked to have been written with her old Parker 25 fountain pen, in her girlish, super-fast, press-so-hard-that-the-nib-bends handwriting. The stamp was slightly skew-whiff, not square with

62

the corner of the envelope, as it would have been if my dad or I had stuck it down.

The seven days between the arrival of the letter and the day she said she would turn up were the longest of my life. I told work that I was off sick, and retired to a darkened room with the intention of spending as much of them as possible asleep. The only way I could avoid nightmares was by getting quietly but stupefyingly drunk.

She arrived, nearly two hours later than she said she would, in a taxi. She was wearing the same red coat with black and gold edging and black hat that she had worn to our wedding – what Kath and some of the guests had referred to as her "Chelsea Pensioner's" outfit. She didn't look dead, or zombie-like. Most fortunately of all, she did not look like the macabre figure she had been in the days leading up to her death. She looked much as I remembered her when she was in her fifties. She was slightly thin and haggard, a state which she had always attributed to overwork, but which had turned out later to be an over-active thyroid gland.

The minute she stepped through the door, she demanded a tour of the house. She poured scorn on every alteration or repair we had made, except a couple which she said she liked, which happened to be the ones we had doubts about ourselves. She was variously appalled at how many of the four hundred bottles I had drunk – she refused to believe that Kath had drunk any of them – and by how few we had bought as replacements. She also went out of her mind when Kath mentioned that she had been looking into selling some of the rarer ones. Do you know what she said? 'Well, I suppose your parents never taught you how to appreciate wine.' I heard a strange noise, and then I realised someone nearby was grinding his teeth, and it was me. She wanted to know where all the antique furniture had gone. It was true that we had sold most of it, because it was impractical and much of it was rather ugly. She demanded to see the auctioneer's receipts, to see how much everything had gone for. I was so shell-shocked that I rooted for them in a drawer and handed them over. She pointed out that an antique German clock had been sold for less than it had cost her to have it renovated. I replied that that is what sometimes happens at auctions, and that German clocks were out of fashion. She called me a feckless idiot, and a philistine.

63

She wanted to know how often we saw Peter. When I said, 'Never,' she wanted to know why. I started to explain to her that her appointing him as an executor had been the sickest, most damaging thing that anyone had ever done to me, and the effect on my mental health was still taking its toll. She told me to pull myself together and not be so soft. She asked about all her other friends. I told her that I had patiently and politely declined most of their advances, because all they ever wanted to do was to talk about her.

She started asking me about work, and about why we did not have any children. I told her I was doing much the same job that I had been doing when she had died. She snorted. I told her that we were an infertile couple. She looked askance at me and Kath in turn, as if trying to evaluate by inspection which one of us was to blame for our barren state.

She asked what we would be having for dinner, and I said I did not know. She started going through the fridge and the kitchen cupboards, but could not find anything to her liking. She complained about the layout of the new kitchen. She asked how we could manage with only one colander. She suggested a trip out to 'The Jade Garden'. I told her that it had closed two years previously. She told me not to be ridiculous, and that 'The Jade Garden' was packed every night and would be the last restaurant in England ever to close.

She went upstairs, stomping her heel on each stair in the way that I just then remembered had always set my teeth on edge, and she inspected the spare bed. She declared that the sheets were insufficiently aired and protested that, just because she was dead, it did not mean that she was not entitled to properly-aired bedding. She asked Kath how often she changed them.

I asked her how long she would be staying. 'Just the one night,' she said, as if that made everything all right, and then, 'I'll be popping back from time to time from now on. I am sorry I left it so long.'

And then there was a knock at the door, and my father arrived. I don't remember much about what happened after that. By the time I woke up, my parents were gone.

The only helpful thing my mother did was to find the deeds. Kath said that she had gone down into the cellar, shaken out the Laura Ashley carrier bag, and there they had been, at the bottom, buried under the love-hearts, the kisses, and the handwritten, elderly pornography.

Here's the letter she sent, if you want to read it. That's my story. Do you think you can help me?

Deleting dadsbooks

Andrew Garner thinks about a solitary evening drink, and is just about to shut down the PC on the oak lending-desk at the Athenian Library, when he notices an email in the inbox.

From: Bernard Snow
To: desk@athenian_library.org.uk
20:38 16 October 2012

Dear Athenian:

As you may remember, my father died just over three years ago. I am sure you do remember it, because of all the trouble we had over my inheritance of his share in the library. Anyway, I did manage to find the subscription document in the end, and so I carry on the membership which he held for so much of his life.

Three years may seem like a long time, but I have only just recently reached the point where I can offer my late father's book collection to the Athenian. It amounts to about 200 volumes, if you include things which I expect have no antiquarian value, such as the old Sotheby's auction catalogues which he was so fond of collecting. It does include some rare first editions, a few of which are signed by the author.

Please let me know if the library wishes to accept the collection as a donation, and any legal formalities which need to be observed.

There are another two paragraphs of rambling about when Mr Snow is likely to be visiting the library again, and a salutation at the end, which Andrew does not read. He forwards the email to one of his personal email addresses, deletes it from the inbox, and deletes the forwarded email from the list of sent items. He looks up Bernard Snow in the members' database, and finds his home telephone number. He notes down his address, which is in a suburb of north Leeds. Andrew locks up and leaves the library, and walks round the corner to a place where he knows there is a working phonebox. He calls Bernard Snow's number.

'Hello? Bernard Snow speaking.'

'Hello, Mr Snow. This is Andrew Garner at the Athenian Library. I just read your email and I wondered if I could come round some time to discuss the matter. The books are located at your house, I take it?'

'Dear me, you are efficient. Yes. The collection is here, where it's always been. Do you want me to come into the library?'

'No, that won't be necessary. If you can let me know your availability, I'll come and see you, and we should be able to complete everything there and then, if that is okay with you.'

'Well, yes – the sooner the better.'

'Is tomorrow evening convenient? Say, seven-thirty?'

'Er, yes. I suppose so. Yes. That's fine.'

'Excellent. I'll see you tomorrow, Mr Snow. Goodbye.'

'What about transport?'

'Sorry?'

'My car's only a hatchback, and I don't know if –'

'Oh, that's all right, Mr Snow. I'll arrange transport. Not to worry. Goodbye.'

Andrew goes to a bar, and drinks the rye whiskey he had been thinking about at the moment when Bernard's email arrived. The whiskey seems tasteless and watery, even though Andrew observed the barman pouring out the measure from a fresh bottle he had just opened. Andrew thinks about the job he has to do the following day, and goes home after just one drink.

*

Andrew parks the plain, white mini-van belonging to the Athenian outside Bernard's house. The house is in a Victorian terrace which is at least one storey higher than the semis on the other side of the street. Andrew rings the doorbell, and peers into the bay window while he is waiting to be let in. He can see a davenport and a bookcase, apparently full of contemporary paperbacks. He hears some footsteps, some loud but indecipherable conversation, and eventually Bernard opens the door, apologetically.

Andrew is reassured as soon as he walks into the sitting room. He does not spend more than a glance on examining the Victorian décor, but goes straight for the two glass-fronted cabinets which Bernard is needlessly telling him house his father's book collection. Andrew notes with relief that the two cabinets are at the back of the room, set into a large alcove, shielded from direct sunlight. He can't help noticing the rubbish that is on top of the cabinets: a glass sweet jar full of seashells, pebbles and water; a tetrahedral terrarium containing some desiccated, brown plant remains, and a few clay objects and pictures in small, cheap frames, made either by a child or an idiot.

'May I?' Andrew asks, as he puts on a new pair of white cotton gloves and turns the brass handle of the first cabinet. Bernard says something about tea, and leaves the room.

Perched on the front of one of the shelves is a box which turns out to be an old 3" x 5" card index. Some of the cards are written in fountain-pen, and some in biro. The fountain-pen writing is small, neat, and very difficult to read. The biro writing is large, untidy, and quite illegible. Andrew realises that both hands belonged to the same person. The cards that Andrew can read are in no apparent order. He picks out a card on which he sees a title he can decipher, *The Apes of God* by Wyndham Lewis. The book is on the shelf. The books, again, do not seem to be in any sort of order. Andrew takes *The Apes of God* off the shelf, and looks inside the front cover. There is a small, embossed, gummed label, with gilt edging. Under the words 'Edition No' is stamped the number 535. He turns over the fly-leaf and looks at the frontispiece. Near the bottom right-hand corner is the author's signature. The edition is dated 1930. That might fetch thirty pounds at a dealer's auction on a bad day, or seven-hundred and fifty pounds to someone with a lot of money and a mania for the work of Wyndham Lewis.

Andrew is scanning the spines of the books when Bernard comes back with the tea-tray.

'I noticed the card index, but I am having a bit of trouble reading it.'

'Yes,' replies Bernard. 'Not surprising, really. You see, he was left-handed, but, when he was at school, that wasn't allowed – manifestation of the devil, and all that nonsense. So they beat him until he wrote with his right hand. The result, as you've just found out, was that his handwriting was like trying to read ancient hieroglyphics. Fortunately, I have been through the books on the shelf and re-catalogued them. I only keep that card index for sentimental reasons. If you'll excuse me a moment, I'll go and fetch it.'

Andrew continues to scan the shelves until Bernard returns again with a battered-looking laptop which seems to work in spite of the low screeching noise coming from inside it. On the screen is a spreadsheet, entitled "dadsbooks". While Bernard pours the tea, Andrew puts a USB pen into the laptop, copies the spreadsheet onto it, and puts it back in his pocket.

Before Andrew can say that they should get down to business, someone pounds on the front door. It sounds like the prelude to a police raid. Bernard goes out again, and is gone for some time. Through the sitting-room door, Andrew hears a muffled conversation with a cheerful man with a West Yorkshire accent, who slams the door after himself after a couple of minutes. Andrew then hears Bernard's half of what sounds like a domestic altercation. Andrew opens the door ajar and listens, but can still only hear what Bernard is saying.

'Yes I know getting the kitchen repaired is important, but so is sorting out the books. I've been trying to get this done for years. Literally years.'

'...'

'YES I KNOW this isn't necessarily the most convenient moment.'

'...'

'Why? Well the library chap seemed very keen. He suggested it.'

'...'

'I didn't WANT to suggest another time. I wanted to get the bloody thing over with. Besides which, it's far better for you to talk to Mr Piggott. You're the one who is always saying that I never get the instructions right. Last time you fell out with me for three days, just because the joiner fitted a door handle at the wrong height – three bloody days.'

'...'

'Yes. Well. I am going back to conclude my transaction with the man from the Athenian.'

'...'

'No, we will not be drinking any alcohol. We will be drinking tea. I have already made some.'

'...'

'YES I KNOW it was my fault I left the grill on, but I will make sure it doesn't happen again.'

'...'

'Well, I'll just have to try not to get drunk again, won't I?'

'...'

'Not listening. Don't start that again. I've got something to attend to.'

Andrew hears purposeful footsteps, and moves back towards the bookcase. Bernard re-enters, looking valiantly cheerful.

'Shall we get down to business?' Bernard asks.

'By all means. Before we start, do you mind if I just ask you why you want to donate the collection? I mean, as opposed to selling it.' Bernard looks perturbed. He sits down, and sips his tea. He puts the teacup down, exhales expansively, closes his eyes, and rubs his temples.

'The effort of dealing with my late parents' estates has exhausted me. It has been almost a full-time occupation for years now, and I can't cope with it any longer. Even if that weren't the case, I would not want the collection to be broken up. My father spent years assembling it. It would seem mercenary to sell it, and I have had it up to here with HMRC, and tax returns, and solicitors. The collection has already been valued for probate, and tax paid. That means that, legally, I can do what I like with it, now. It might sound strange, but I don't want to give the Revenue the satisfaction of re-charging me if it went at auction for more than the value of the probate assessment. I just want it done with. And, well, we had a bit of an accident in the kitchen, recently. It nearly caused a fire. That gave me a jolt. I decided that the collection had to go straight away to a safe place, where it could be looked after by experts and scholars. My dad was a member of the Athenian for over forty years, and so it seemed obvious what I should do.' Bernard glances at Andrew's white cotton gloves. 'And what is the point of books that you have to take so much trouble to handle? Books to me are about words and meaning, not being a small-print-run, manufactured object which is intended just to sit in a cabinet and get valuable.'

'Do you mind if I ask who did the probate assessment?'

'That was funny. I sent an email to an auction house. I forget which one, but one of the well-known ones. I included the catalogue in that spreadsheet as an attachment. They said that the total value of the collection was not big enough for it to be worth their while to auction it, and so they were sorry, but there was no help they could offer me. But they sent the spreadsheet back and, when I looked at it, I saw that they had added a "value" column, which had what seemed to be a reasonable figure for each item, which was all I had asked them for. They didn't charge me a fee.'

Andrew glances at the laptop screen, and scrolls down to the row for *Finnegan's Wake*, signed by James Joyce. The valuation is £3,000 to £6,000. Andrew considers that is a reasonable valuation, but he could also think of potential buyers who would pay well over £100,000 for it, depending on the precise details of its condition, the state of the market at that moment, and whether the buyer liked the serial number. Only 425 copies were ever signed. Andrew hopes this one has a three-digit number, preferably with two 8s in it: that would appeal to the Chinese market.

'Would you want to see them regularly, when you went to visit the Athenian?' asks Andrew.

'No. Not me. I might possibly be interested to hear any news about other people wanting to see them, or study them, under proper, scholarly conditions, but I don't intend to see them again. I just want to move on. Assembling this collection was my father's project, but I don't want to assume the responsibility of having to safeguard it myself. By accepting it, particularly as a complete lot, the Athenian would be doing me a great favour. I presume there will have to be a deed of gift.'

'A deed of gift, yes.'

'I was thinking the deed of gift could just be a letter, in hard copy, signed by me, addressed to the Chief Librarian.'

'Yes. That is exactly what I was thinking.'

'Shall I go and print one now?'

'Yes, of course. By all means. Do you need the laptop back?'

'No. There's a computer upstairs. I'll just go and print it off now.'

'Do you mind if I get some chests out of the van, and start packing the collection up?'

'Oh, you've brought a van? Splendid. No, I don't mind at all. You just carry on.'

Andrew has already begun to evaluate which items he is going to put in Box 1, which in Box 2, and which under "miscellaneous junk".

Bernard returns with the letter. Andrew stops packing for a moment to peer over Bernard's shoulder as he signs, folds the letter into thirds, puts it into an envelope, and hands it to Andrew. Andrew has hardly had time to pack anything yet. He has got as far as the *Finnegan's Wake*; a signed, numbered copy of Durrell's *Alexandrine Quartet*, and another signed, numbered copy of *Trembling of the Veil* by W. B. Yeats. The next is *On the Frontier* by W. H. Auden and Christopher Isherwood. The dust jacket is slightly soiled, but it is signed by Auden and it should be worth at least four hundred and fifty pounds.

As Andrew steadily fills Box 1, he finds he has to suppress a laugh.

'Is something the matter?' asks Bernard, who paces up and down, and fiddles with the tea-set.

'No, not at all. I just get a bit nervous when I am handling so many folios like these.'

'Ah. Of course.'

The last item Andrew puts into Box 1 is an unsigned but mint condition copy of a pamphlet by Dorothy L. Sayers, called *The Other Six Deadly Sins*, containing the text of a lecture the crime novelist gave to something called The Public Morality Council in 1941. This does not take up much space, and Andrew admits to himself that he has no idea how to value it without consulting sources beyond his own knowledge and instinct. He thinks there might be a chance that some fool could mistake it for a previously unknown Lord Peter Wimsey story.

Box 2 has no signed copies in it, and contains more popular stuff with larger print runs, such as J. B. Priestley's *An Inspector Calls*. Andrew recalls from the spreadsheet that the venerable father had paid ten shillings for this, and that ten shillings would be worth substantially more if it had been deposited in a savings account in the same year, and just left to accumulate. Box 2 also contains what would otherwise have been candidates for Box 1, had the vicissitudes of time and human mishandling not removed or torn the dust jacket, loosened the pages, or broken the spine.

The other chests contain the items which are simply not worth selling, and which Andrew would happily inflict on a charity shop if it were not for the fact that he wants no witnesses – certainly no witnesses other than Bernard. Andrew can hardly help looking distastefully at the laden shelves of old Sotheby's catalogues which Bernard had forewarned him about in the email. They weigh a ton, and cannot possibly be of any value to anybody. Andrew dutifully places them in chests and carries them out to the van. He has a brief rest before returning each time.

Andrew comes back into the sitting room to find Bernard taking a decanter out of the sideboard.

'I would offer you a whisky, but of course you are driving.'

'Yes. I'm fine. Nothing for me, thanks.'

'Glass of water? More tea? Orange juice?'

'No, I am absolutely fine. I must be on my way now that the van is packed.' Bernard regards the varnished wood of the shelves, as dark and shiny as bonfire toffee, which has been revealed by the sacking of the glass-fronted cabinets. The sight seems to make the whole room seem emptier, but he sighs contentedly. He thought he would never get this job done, and now it is on the verge of completion. He has hundreds of books that he wants to read, in boxes, in the attic. He looks forward to selecting the ones to restock the liberated glass cabinets.

'He was a great scholar of English, you know, my father,' says Bernard. Andrew shifts his weight from one foot to the other.

'I have no doubt.'

'This is the house where I grew up.'

'Fascinating. Well, I must be going, now. I've got to take the van back to the garage, you see. Goodbye.'

'Yes, of course. Well, drive carefully.'

Andrew doesn't hear Bernard wishing him goodnight from the doorway as he drives away. He puts his foot down, heads into the city centre and takes the southbound M1 to Wakefield. He drives to a secluded spot he knows among some vacant units on an industrial estate by the banks of the river Calder. He parks in semi-darkness in front of a row of derelict garages. By the light of an electric torch, he opens the back doors of the van and takes out everything except Boxes 1 and 2. He double-checks these to make sure he has made no mistake as to which they are, and locks the van.

Andrew takes out a bunch of keys, and opens the padlock on one of the old garages. He can just about see inside, because most of the roof has caved in. He closes the door behind him, and turns the torch on, to avoid tripping over the broken pieces of asbestos. Inside the garage is a wire basket incinerator, perched on two piles of bricks. He considered getting rid of the unwanted material by throwing it in the river, but the bank is too steep and muddy to drive the van down, and the books are too heavy for him to carry all the way down to the water's edge from where the van is parked. The incinerator it will have to be, even though it is more conspicuous.

He picks up a light volume, which happens to be *Great Morning* by Osbert Sitwell, catalogue price: one pound, and tears it apart for kindling. He follows this with a uselessly shabby copy of *Point-Counterpoint* by Aldous Huxley, and half a dozen others, which he doesn't bother to examine. Some of them aren't even first editions.

The Sotheby's catalogues are dense, glossy and look forbiddingly non-flammable. There are too many of them for him to tear up. He shines the torch on the pile of wood that he keeps as a reserve, mostly old pallets which he has broken up with an axe, and a pine bunk-bed that his next-door neighbour was getting rid of, and let him have for nothing. He makes a neat pile of the planks which he has stored in the dryish spot under the remaining intact part of the garage roof. He leaves plenty of gaps for air to circulate through. The final arrangement looks like that outsize, idiotic version of jenga that students play in pubs. Andrew unscrews the cap on the plastic jerry can full of petrol, and pours some over the torn remains of *Great Morning* and *Point-Counterpoint*. He throws on a lighted match and waits for the wood to catch fire.

As soon as the wood has properly taken, he opens the first Sotheby's catalogue, entitled *1980: Important European Arms and Armour*, and spreads it out, roughly from the middle. He places it delicately on top of the pyre. For one moment it looks as if it is just going to lie there inertly, but then a black ring starts to move inwards across the cover from the corners, and the laminated covering of the catalogue starts to bubble and char. After a minute, it is sufficiently consumed for Andrew to pick up the next one. Extrapolating from how long it took the first one to burn, he reckons he can get through all of them in about 90 minutes.

Andrew stands in the glow of the fire, his cheeks red, his clothes absorbing the smell of smoke, and starts to feel sleepy with the lateness of the hour, and the monotony of waiting for the previous volume to catch fully alight before putting the next one on. There is a rumble and a flurry of sparks as the weakening structure of the charred pine planks rearranges itself under its own weight. A fragment of glossy paper spins upwards towards the hole in the roof. Andrew thinks he can make out a glimpse of a nude, alabaster Venus, looking into a mirror. He wonders how much it fetched at auction. The burning fragment is taken by the breeze and is gone. Andrew does not worry whether it survives his attempt to incinerate it. That fragment on its own is not enough to fix anything on him. He has already decided that he will be leaving the Athenian and the name Andrew Garner behind in a few days.

He thinks about potential buyers from the Far East, Arabia, and North America. He also tries to work out how long it will take him to sell the contents of Box 2, judiciously blended with some of his own stock, and possibly a few of the less conspicuous items from the Athenian's deeper recesses, at Bonham's, Christie's, or even bloody Sotheby's with their Kryptonite catalogues.

His cheeks are still red from the fire, but his feet and his back are getting cold. He wishes he had some of the whisky that had been offered to him earlier.

The last thing he pushes into the fire is the deed of gift, first the envelope and then the letter. He smashes the blackened leaf of the letter with a stick, pisses on the embers, and drives back to his flat.

*

Bernard, his second whisky in his hand, is still looking inside the empty cabinets. They had been filled to capacity for his whole life, and he had never realised that the shelves were adjustable, with wooden pegs. He finishes his drink, and wonders if he should move his reference books from upstairs into this room.

He goes over to the laptop on the table. The screen says, "Confirm deletion of file dadsbooks.xls?" Bernard clicks "Yes".

He downs the whisky and pours another. Just a small one. He goes into the kitchen, which, like most of the rest of the house, is in darkness, his wife having gone to bed. He turns on a slow trickle of water from the tap, and holds the glass underneath it. He turns the tap on full, pours the whisky down the sink, rinses the glass, and goes upstairs to bed.

As he ascends, he decides he will relinquish his membership of the Athenian, so that someone else can make fuller use of it, and he will take his wife to the theatre at the weekend.

Axe-woman

My name is Elspeth. I won't tell you how old I am in years, but I will say that, when I was born, number 1 in the charts was 'Yellow Submarine' by the Beatles. When I was conceived, it was 'All You Need Is Love'. Lester, my husband, who left me about six weeks ago, is a few years younger than me. When he was conceived, number 1 was 'So Here It Is Merry Christmas' by Slade, and when he was born, it was 'Mama We're All Crazee Now', which is a fair summary of our marriage.

Lester called himself a musician. He never made any money out of it. I'm a management accountant for a network engineering firm. It pays the bills. At least, it used to. They put me down to three days a week recently. I haven't got round to working out if I can still get by, yet. That's unusual for me. I like to stay on top of things like bills and rent and bank statements.

Lester never told me he was leaving, which was typical of him.

We'd had a few big rows over the last year or two, and once or twice I'd thrown him out, or he'd gone off in a huff, and come back the following day, as soon as he'd run out of money, still drunk or stoned or in the early stage of a hangover. There was one time when I was in the hallway when he let himself in – I hadn't deadlocked the door – and as soon as I saw him, I realised he was still blathered and he'd pissed his trousers, his favourite mustardy-coloured jeans with the purple patches on. I pointed at his damp groin and laughed. He barged past me into the kitchenette, took forty quid out of the tea caddy, and barged out again, still piss-stained. That was one of the moments when I realised it couldn't carry on.

This time, I just came back from work – it happened to be the day they told me they were cutting my hours from full-time down to three days a week – and he wasn't here. My first thought was that he'd just gone to the pub. I looked in the tea caddy, and saw it was empty. Next, I thought how unreasonable it was of him to go to the pub on a Tuesday tea-time, and then I went online to check my bank accounts. Lester only had access to the joint account. I have no idea why we had a joint account. My salary was never paid into it, but I used to transfer three hundred and fifty pounds a month for "household expenses". Lester had cleared it out. That was when I realised that, whether he was at the pub or somewhere else, he wasn't coming back that night.

It was difficult to tell how much stuff Lester had taken with him, except that it can't have been more than would fit in an overnight bag. After two or three days, I had tidied the flat so that it was in a better state than it had been since we moved in. After a week, I started taking some of Lester's more disgusting old clothes to the dump – most of them weren't fit for a charity shop, even the ones he hadn't pissed or shat himself in or thrown-up over. And his books. They were mostly stuff like *The Tao of Physics*, *Zen and the Art of Motorcycle Maintenance*, and bloody *Lord of the Rings*. He must have had six copies of that, in various states of falling to pieces. One of them was a hardback in a large format, in good condition, with colour pictures. The pictures looked like album covers for some prog rock outfit like Magnum or Yes. I put that on eBay, and got fifteen quid for it. I got a total of sixty-five quid for his Warhammer books and another sixty for the little men that he used to spend hours painting when he was in a strop and wasn't talking to me.

The one set of stuff of Lester's that I kept was his electric guitar and amp, and all the things that went with it: leads, strap, case, plectrums, electronic tuner, spare strings, and some music books. Lester never knew it, but, even before he walked out, I had sometimes had a go at playing the guitar on the odd occasions when I was in the flat during the day and he happened to be out. I didn't play it at night, which was usually when Lester left me on my own, because our landlord, Mr Bradfield, lives in the house next door to us, and he has a thing about noise. He sometimes used to bang on the wall when Lester and I were having a row. He even came to the door a couple of times. So we used to have rows without shouting. They were still rows. Worse than the usual, shouty rows in some ways.

The guitar is the most expensive thing that Lester owned, even including the van, which is legally half mine, and on which I have had the ignition lock changed, just like the lock on the door of the flat. It's a Gibson Les Paul "Studio", with a cherry-red finish and a rosewood fret-board. It's the only pricey thing he ever bought from a proper shop, rather than some scabby bloke in the pub. He paid for it with some money he earned from doing a delivery job. The amp is nothing

77

to write home about. It's a Laney Mighty 8. The 8 means eight watts of power. A normal studio amp would be 50 watts, but even 8 is more than loud enough to annoy Mr Bradfield.

Lester used to call this guitar his "axe". Well, it's my axe, now.

I find practising the guitar is an OK way of passing the time I would be spending in the office if they had not cut my hours. I get up at the same time I usually do for work, get washed and dressed and have breakfast as normal, except in tattier clothes, and then start practising. I make a point of washing and drying my hands thoroughly before I start. I find it keeps the strings cleaner and makes them last longer. Now that I have been doing at least two solid days practice a week for a few weeks, I find I am actually starting to sound as if I can play.

In my morning session, I keep the amp very low, and listen to it through headphones, and I practice scales and new chord positions. When I learn a new chord, I first practice playing it cleanly – getting all the strings pressed down to the fretboard so that they don't buzz, or sound muffled. When I have got the hang of strumming the chord with a clean sound, I practice changing between the new chord and another one that I can already play. To start with, I just change back and forth, back and forth, between two chords, say E minor and B7, over and over again. I might practice the same chord change a hundred times, before my hands get too tired and I need a little rest. I found at first that I had to cut my fingernails very short on my left hand, and my fingertips got very sore and bled occasionally. They have hardened-up now. I don't find playing even a bit uncomfortable any more. You might think that playing the same chord change a hundred times would be dreary and monotonous, but I find it relaxing. I also find it is helping me to develop an ear for which chords sound good together. One of the books Lester left behind is about music theory. I've read most of it, but I find it only makes sense if I can hear something that shows what the theory is on about.

After lunch, I take the headphones off and turn the amp up a notch or two, which I think is perfectly reasonable. From my flat, I can hear other people vacuuming and things, so why shouldn't I turn my amp up a bit? My afternoon session is when I try to learn some songs. I never turn the amp up higher than number 5. Mr Bradfield has tapped on the wall a few times, but he has not come to the door yet. If he starts banging, I either have a break, or turn the amp back down. It can be frustrating, especially if I'm just getting into a new piece and it's something really rocking.

I've been trying a bit of lead guitar recently. I've been listening to the cover version of *Walk on By* by The Stranglers. I love the guitar solo. I think I am ready to have a go at copying it.

Today is Thursday, one of my days off. I have got my guitar all set up, and I've tuned it. That takes me a lot less time now that it used to, and I've got out of the habit of snapping the strings. I've recorded the *Walk on By* track off the CD onto an old-fashioned audio cassette. I've got the cassette player on the coffee table next to me. I'm going to play the solo, pausing the tape at the end of each phrase, and rewind and re-listen to it as many times as it takes me to get each one. Each time I get a phrase right, I'll play what I've learned again from the beginning. I'll keep doing that until I can play the whole solo.

I'll be starting a band, soon, at this rate.

The first bit is not too difficult, but it is not long before I have to do a string bend. Fortunately, it's on the high E string, which is the thinnest and so the easiest to bend. I'm still getting the hang of string bending. I fret the note as usual, but then I have to push the string up the fretboard to stretch it. It makes the note higher when I push up, and lower again as I move my finger back again. It takes a lot of force. I'm glad the fingertips on my left hand are already toughened-up.

This isn't really getting anywhere. To get the full effect of the string bending, I need more of a sustained sound, and that means more volume. When I listen with the headphones, if I turn the amp up to more than about number 6, I get a headache. I need the sound to go through the amp's main speaker, and I need to pump it up. I turn it up to number 7. I know it's only 10am. Ah, this is more like it. For the next bit, I need to hammer-on. That is when you strike a note, and then you bring another finger down onto the fretboard, to strike a higher note on the same string, but without plucking the string again. It only works if you bring your second finger down very hard, which is why they call it hammering-on.

Bloody hell. That's the door.

I put my guitar down, look through the spy-hole and, sure enough, I can see Mr Bradfield. I open the door.

'What are you playing at?'

'*Walk on By* by The Stranglers.'

'What?'

'I'm working out the guitar solo from The Stranglers' cover version of *Walk on By*, if you want to know.'

'Who is?'

'Who is what?'

'Who is making that bloody racket?'

'I am. Well, I was. I had to stop when I heard someone at the door.'

'You are?'

'Yes.'

'Where's your husband?'

'What has that got to do with your complaint about the noise?'

'I thought it was your husband who is the musician and makes all the row.'

'So did he. It used to be him, but now it's me.'

'So where is your husband?'

'I've no idea. He left about six weeks ago, and didn't say where he would be going.' Mr Bradfield can't think of anything to say to that. He looks as if he doesn't believe me.

'You stop that bloody row - playing loud guitars at ten o'clock in the morning. I'm not having it.' He turns and goes back downstairs. I shut the door. I give Mr Bradfield half an hour to cool off while I have a cup of tea and a Jaffa Cake, and then I begin practising my solo again, still without the headphones.

I have just settled into it again when the sound from the amp dies. I fiddle with the on-off switch. I wonder if the fuse in the plug might have blown, and so I go to the kitchenette to get the little screwdriver out of the cutlery drawer, and I notice that the fridge has stopped buzzing and the display on the microwave has gone off. I try the light switch. Nothing. Mr Bradfield has turned the power off.

I get ready to go out. I don't know why, but, as I'm taking my slippers off, I have an impulse to put flat shoes on to go out in. I root around in the cupboard and find my old Doc Marten's, which I haven't worn for years.

I go downstairs, and out into the street. Mr Bradfield's house has a secure entry system on the front door. There is no way I am going to ring the bell of Mr Bradfield's flat because I don't want him to know that I know that the fuse box for both his house and my house is in his cellar. I loiter around in the street for quite a while. Eventually, I see a young woman in the porch of Mr Bradfield's house. She's coming out. She's got a child in a buggy with her. I rush up the steps and she opens the front door. I help her with the buggy. I prop the door open with the doormat. I help the woman all the way down to the pavement, and then I go into Mr Bradfield's house and down into the cellar.

The box doesn't have old-fashioned fuses: it's a new one with circuit-breakers and switches. Sure enough, every switch on the board is in the up position, except the one labelled "No 17 – top floor". I flick the switch back on.

I get back upstairs to my landing and I realise that I left my door on the latch, which is fortunate in a way, because I didn't bring my keys with me, but I also see that the door of my flat is now ajar. I stand just outside the door and listen. I can hear someone moving stuff around. Now they are doing up a zip. It sounds like the zip of my guitar case. I go inside.

It's Lester. He has the guitar case in one hand and the carrying-handle of the amplifier in the other. While he has no hands free, I grab him round the throat, and knee him in the groin. He bends at the waist and his knees buckle. Without letting go of his throat, I knee him again, and then jam one foot against the inside of his foot to give me a levering-point before I push him over. He goes down underneath me. He cracks the back of his head on the edge of the dining table as he goes down, and unintentionally butts me in the face under the impact. I can feel my bottom lip start to swell and I can taste my own blood. There is a satisfying crunch as I land on top of Lester. I suffer no damage from the fall, because I use his body as a cushion. His head is under the dining table, in exactly the position mine was when we had sex on this floor, the same day we moved into the flat. I grab his throat again. He's winded. His eyes look as if they are about to pop out as I squeeze harder. He tries to push me off, but there is no strength in his arms. All he can do is flap his hands against me. I squeeze, and squeeze, and squeeze. I'm rubbing my crotch against him. The throat-squeezing isn't working, and so I dig my fingers in. I can feel the cartilage in his throat start to crack. I rub my crotch against his thigh harder and faster. His eyes open even wider. I'm getting really turned on. Lester's eyes are still staring, wide open. I've never seen anyone's eyes open so wide. I know that I just have to keep going for a little longer. I can feel myself starting to come. I reach full climax at just the moment he starts to die. I want him to die, but I don't want his death to be over too soon.

I have come so hard that I have to lie on top of the body for a few minutes to recover. I get up rather unsteadily. I am about unzip the case to check that my guitar is okay, but then I pause to wash my hands and dry them first. And then I go back to examine my guitar.

There is a knock at the door. I don't bother to look to see who it is.

'Yes?'

'Now what manner of racket are you making? It sounded like a fight.'

'Yes. It was a fight. It's over now.' Mr Bradfield looks over my shoulder and sees Lester's body. I can tell Mr Bradfield is going to try to barge past me. I think I have a surprise for him. I turn sideways so that he can get past without touching me. He does touch me. He doesn't have to, but he does.

Mr Bradfield kneels down next to the body and peers at it.

'Forgive me, Les Paul, wherever you are,' I say out loud, as I swing my guitar by the beautiful, rosewood fretboard so that the edge of the guitar's body hits Mr Bradfield on the back of his skull. He topples over, unconscious.

I put on the rubber gloves I use to do the washing-up, so that my skin won't have to touch Mr Bradfield's greasy outer coating, and I bind his wrists and his ankles together with parcel tape which I managed to find in the cupboard under the sink. Halfway through doing his ankles, I run out of parcel tape, and so I finish the job with Elastoplast strip from the bathroom cupboard. I feel the back of his head to see if I have broken any bones, but I can't feel anything out of order. I put the kettle on and have another Jaffa Cake while I am waiting for Mr Bradfield to regain consciousness. I get a plastic bag out of the kitchen cupboard and cut two large holes in it. I place it over Mr Bradfield's head just as he is waking up. It is not to suffocate him: it is just to cover up his ugly face, except for his eyes. I tie the handles of the bag around his neck, just to keep the bag in position.

I lie down on top of Mr Bradfield, with one of his legs in my crotch, and I start to rub myself against him. I put my hands round his throat and squeeze. I can see his eyes start to bulge, and I can feel myself getting turned on. I am determined not to have to dig my fingers in this time. I put more energy into squeezing and less into humping. The

82

eyes bulge more and more. I am just on the edge of climax, and I give a harder squeeze, and Mr Bradfield's eyes go a millimetre wider than Lester's did. That is when I start to come. Instead of crying out, I squeeze convulsively, and I feel Mr Bradfield die, which makes me come all over again.

I roll off the body and lie looking up at the ceiling for a few minutes. I wonder how often they'll let me play the guitar in prison. I wonder if I should turn myself in.

No, sod that. I know what I'm going to do. I'm going to go on the run. They'll freeze my bank account once they've worked out it's me, I suppose, and so I'd better get some cash out before I set off. I empty Lester's wallet and find it has a hundred-and-eighty pounds in it – presumably what's left from the joint account – and an unclaimed scratch card which has won fifty quid.

I wonder if I would enjoy mutilating Lester's and Mr Bradfield's bodies. I love it when their eyes start to pop out, and I like them to know who's doing it to them. I think that's the bit that turns me on so much. I might as well go next door and do Mrs Bradfield as well, when she gets back from work. I wonder if I'll still come as hard when I'm killing a woman.

Cut

My name is Molly. That's short for molybdenum. I'm mostly made of iron and plastic, but part of me is a metal called molybdenum. My handle is orange. My blade is 88 millimetres long, single-edged and pointed. I'm not serrated. Serration is for poofs. I can go for a very long time without needing to be sharpened. A very long time. I'm light and well-balanced.

I have just been picked up by a young man. Quite an attractive young man. He doesn't look like the usual sort of customer in this market. He has long hair and spectacles, and looks like a student. At least his hair seems quite clean. He spends ages and ages looking over every item on this stall. He puts me into a cheap, aluminium colander, and the colander into a red, plastic washing-up bowl. He also buys a pair of nutcrackers, and a frying pan and a saucepan which I could tell him will not be his friends: their metal is too thin.

His name is Henry. I find that out when we get home. He is indeed a student. He is about to go to Liverpool University. He bought me because he will be living in a self-catering house instead of the usual hall of residence. His mother asks him a lot of questions about whether he will be able to look after himself. Henry says that he has been cooking all his own meals since he was fourteen years old. His mother says that she always cooks the Sunday dinner. Henry concedes this, and says that he has been cooking all his own meals since he was fourteen years old, including his breakfast seven days a week, except the Sunday dinner. I can tell when he is starting to get annoyed. I quite like him when he is annoyed.

We have arrived in Liverpool. Henry has been out on his first food shopping expedition. I can't wait to see what he has brought back. I would like it to include a two-rib beef roast, but I know that that is way outside Henry's price range. I'd settle for a Gressingham duck – that's surprisingly economical. Or a piece of pork shoulder with crackling that needs scoring. Or a chicken that needs jointing. Or a piece of lamb leg that he wants to cut into cubes prior to marinating and making into kebabs. Or fish. Uncooked prawns in shell that need slitting and the digestive canal removing. Plaice, or cod, or haddock that needs filleting. Slabs of tuna that need cutting into just the right thickness for the griddle-pan.

He has brought three shopping bags into the kitchen, each one full to overflowing. He takes out: a floret of broccoli, a bag of potatoes, and a cauliflower. He takes out a punnet of mushrooms, three packets of tofu, a bag of cashew nuts, and a bottle of tamari. He takes out a packet of some kind of sausage-meat substitute, a packet of lemon verbena tea, a bag of brown rice, and three cartons of soya milk. He takes out various tins with plastic lids, which contain spices, and then bags of chapatti flour and bottles of sunflower oil, olive oil, grapeseed oil, and sesame oil.

I can't cut oil. Oh my god. I've ended up with a vegan. How am I going to get out of this?

My first job with Henry is to slice one of his flabby, weeping slabs of tofu. I'm sobbing all the while. You brought me all this way for this. You don't need a knife: you could cut this stuff with a strip torn from the one hundred per cent recycled cardboard box it came in.

Somehow, I get through it. I'm still sharp. Henry holds me in his left hand, and scrapes his right thumb over my cutting edge, and I can tell he is impressed. I'll make a cutter of him, yet.

Henry's girlfriend has come to stay. She is not a foodie. She moans constantly about her weight and chides Henry every time he opens the top of the bottle of sunflower oil. Sunflower oil for Christ's sake. Henry is cooking their dinner. Homemade wholemeal pizza base with homemade tomato sauce, green peppers, mushrooms, and herbs. Even the girlfriend eats it without complaint. The other students who share the house come into the kitchen and ask Henry if he has considered a part-time job at Pizza Hut. They aren't joking. I cut the onions, the mushrooms, and the peppers. That was all. I think I may be allergic to peppers.

The girlfriend goes home. She is a year behind Henry, because she failed her 'A' levels. If she passes next time, she is going to apply to Liverpool Institute of Higher Education, just so she can be in the same city as Henry. I have heard Henry praying that she will fail again. I heard her say that she was too rubbish for him, and that she had to split up with him, and I saw him do a kind of Maradona goal celebration while he was on his way to the toilet and the girlfriend was still in bed. But they are still together. The girlfriend has told Henry that she doesn't see the two of them as ideal partners, but she 'wants to keep an eye on him'. Henry did not reply, but the expression on his face was the same one I saw when his mother was going on about whether he would be able to cook his own meals.

Every night I try. 'Eat meat. Carve meat. Give me blood, bone, and sinews.' Every night. So far, I have not got through to him.

She has come to stay again. Henry meets her at Lime Street station. They eat tofu and brown rice. They go to bed. They shag. They shag more loudly than is perhaps necessary. They get up. They have a frugal, whole-grain, low-fat, low-cholesterol, no-added-salt-or-sugar vegan breakfast. Henry does the washing up while the girlfriend eats a box of liqueur chocolates.

They are so tired from shagging that they have an early night. During the night, Henry wakes up. He gets out of bed, walks into the kitchen, and takes me out of the drawer.

He takes me back into the bedroom. The girlfriend is asleep, on her front. I can hear her gentle snoring. Henry grabs my handle. Oh, no. No. This is not what I had in mind.

Henry moves my blade closer and closer to her back. I am over her scapulae, her lungs, her spinal column. Henry cuts a label off the girlfriend's bra, which she wears even in bed, and throws it onto the bedroom floor. He gets back into bed beside her, and hugs her, with an expression of passing relief on his face.

Henry has graduated and is single again. He is moving into a bedsit in Glasgow, prior to starting his PhD. His mother drove us here. I don't know where the girlfriend ended up. I think she got off with a bloke from Birmingham.

It is late, but Henry goes out to have a look at the local shops. He comes back with a laden carrier bag. He takes a frying pan out of one of the boxes, and puts it on the hob. He takes something out of the carrier bag, and picks me up. I'm slicing through plastic. I can smell bacon. He has bought a sliced white loaf, two packets of rindless, back bacon, a packet of butter – not vegan margarine – real butter, and a bottle of HP sauce. He makes himself a large mug of strong tea with cow's milk, and a six-rasher bacon sandwich, with bacon fat and sauce running out of it. He eats it standing up in the kitchen, as it gets dark.

On Saturday, Henry buys a leg of lamb. He has also bought a carving knife. I wish I had a longer blade. He has cooked the meat to perfection. The skin is crisp. We have finished chopping the greens: he uses me to test the spitting joint when he takes it out of the oven. It is still pink in the middle, and I taste blood. That is all I get, because the cooking is finished. He uses the other knife to do the carving.

He goes to bed not long after he has finished his roast lamb dinner. He leaves the joint in the roasting tin and abandons the washing-up. He is still not reaccustomed to heavy, fat- and protein-rich meals. They make him sleepy.

Henry wakes in the middle of the night. He pours salt over the leftover roast, picks me up off the counter, and has another stand-up meal, using me to carve strips which he devours, one by one. I can feel the bone. Henry scrapes me up and down it. I almost get stuck and Henry nearly ends up swallowing a splinter of bone. He puts me down, picks up the bone in both hands, and gnaws it. He sprinkles more salt, and gnaws again. He takes a piece of bread and mops up the bouillon and the congealed fat in the bottom of the roasting tin. He squirts washing-up liquid into a bowl, and runs water into it. The immersion heater has not been on, and so the water is cold. I spend the next 18 hours in a bowl of cold, fatty, frothy water with the roasting tin and other utensils, including the new carving knife.

The week after, he has roast pork. He uses me to score the skin of the raw joint, but the new knife gets to do the carving. He has chicken and steak and sausages through the week, and roast beef on Sunday. I don't get to touch the beef at all, not even after it has gone cold. He usually likes his meat really well done on the outside, and virtually raw in the middle, which is just the way I like it. I am upset about the beef. I wish my blade had been at least another 60 millimetres long. We shorter knives have to do the veg, and the tofu, and open the packets of bacon, but we only get to touch the meat occasionally, and usually only when it's raw. We only get to carve the cooked meat once it has gone cold. It has been good to touch bone. I shouldn't complain. Even cold meat is better than tofu. I really shouldn't complain.

It has been three weeks since I touched meat, apart from Henry's hand. I peel potatoes. I peel carrots. I peel parsnips. I slice cabbage and chop courgettes. I hate courgettes. I'm even more allergic to courgettes than I am to peppers. They taste like cotton wool soaked in washing-up water. The only thing I hate more than courgettes is butternut squash. I chop butternut squash. I cut Henry's thumb. I think I'm doing okay one minute, but then I do it without thinking. I regret it for a moment, but then I'm glad. The cut is deep and open, with a large flap of skin hanging off it. Henry looks stupidly at the chunks of veg on the chopping board, red with blood. He looks at the cut. He looks around as if in a daze for something to use to staunch the flow. He tries to tear off some sheets of kitchen paper with one hand, but only succeeds in unfurling the whole roll. He hasn't got any sticking plaster. He has to phone a work colleague to bring some round. He abandons his food preparation and retires to the sofa. He complains of feeling dizzy and sick. I don't feel in the least bit dizzy, but I am starting to feel sick.

I am in a packing case, in a storage unit back in Henry's home town. I've been here for weeks. Henry bought a set of Sabatier knives after he got the news about his new job. The carving knife he had in Glasgow isn't in here. He decided to take it with him to his new house.

Can We Have You All Sitting Down, Please?

My name is Mason Bentley. I'm a student at Stainbeck College of Tertiary Education. I do maths, geology, and information and communication technology. ICT is my favourite lesson. The teacher is called Mr Woolley.

I am at my desk, and I can see Mr Woolley now, peering through the safety glass panel in the door of the classroom. The students have all arrived – those that can be bothered to turn up. Mr Woolley arrives last, and his face is red and a bit sweaty, as usual.

Mr Woolley can be funny, sometimes. This is the first funny thing about him: how long it takes him to get into the classroom. He looks as if he is counting how many people he can see inside. I don't mean counting like teachers count when they want to know how many sheets or how many books to hand out. It is more like the way I would look at a group of teenagers hanging around the entrance to a subway. Then he just stands there for a moment, holding his briefcase and the files he keeps the lesson in. I don't know what he is doing while he stands there. He puts his briefcase down, turns the door handle with his free hand, and pushes the briefcase through the door in front of him with this foot. Most of the students don't notice him: they just carry on with whatever they are doing.

He puts his stuff down on the teacher's desk, and says, 'Can we have you all sitting down, please?' He says it in his normal voice, which is not very loud. The only person who hears him is me. I line my notepad up with the edge of the desk, and I put my pen next to the pad, and I look at Mr Woolley to let him know that I'm listening to him, but he is not looking at me. He is looking at Jade Kennington, Gilbert Owusu, and Aaron Braithwaite. They are standing up, or sitting astride their chairs, with their backs to him, arguing over something on someone's smart phone – I think it is an app that one of them has downloaded. 'Can we have you all sitting down, please?' He says it again, a bit louder.

'Listen to this cool app,' says Jade. She presses a button on her smart phone. The speaker makes some noise that I don't believe anybody could recognise or understand: it just sounds like a random crackle.

89

'What is it?' asks Gilbert.

'It's an app that says "Shut up!" in fifty different languages.'

'What was that one?' asks Gilbert Owusu.

'Ukra. Ukree-ann-ian. Something foreign,' say Jade. Gilbert guffaws.

'Give it here,' he says, and tries to grab the phone from Jade's hand.

'Can we have you all sitting down, please? Can we have you all sitting down, please?' Mr Woolley says it still a bit louder.

'What's the point of telling someone to shut up in a language they can't understand?' says Gilbert.

'Oh, never mind. It's just a cool app – that's all.'

'Can we have you all sitting down and facing the front, please?' Now they go and sit down, slowly. It is difficult to tell if they sit down because of what Mr Woolley said, or if they just decided they were going to do it anyway.

Mr Woolley goes quiet for a bit, and puts his files, and his ring-binders, and the wooden box he keeps his pens in, on the desk. People start whispering and talking again. Jade Kennington has started another conversation. As she talks, she brushes her hair and looks at herself in a mirror she has placed on the desk in front of her.

Usually, Mr Woolley has a file in front of him in the middle of the desk with the day's lesson in it. Last week we did "packet switching", which I think we should be doing again today, because it is quite an important topic. Today, he has two files: one on the left and one on the right. He looks from one to the other. He holds his hand over the files. He wiggles his hand from side to side, as if he has just burnt his finger, but it is a long time before he picks one up. He picks up the right-hand file. He moves the file to the centre of the desk, opens it, and then goes to the whiteboard and starts drawing a diagram about packet switching. I write the date at the top of a new page, and start copying the diagram onto my notepad. Mr Woolley explains the diagram, but I can't hear all of what he is saying because Jade Kennington is having an argument with the person sitting behind her.

Mr Woolley has stopped talking and is looking at us, at the class. I look at his eyes, which appear big behind the lenses of his glasses, and I try to work out who he is looking at. He looks at Jade. He looks at Aaron Braithwaite, and then he looks back to Jade. Both Jade and

Aaron are concentrating on their smart phones. Mr Woolley puts down his marker pen and watches them.

He stands in front of the whiteboard, quite still. He doesn't usually do this. He either sits behind the teacher's desk, or he moves between the desk and the whiteboard, bouncing from one to the other like one of those little wind-up bumper cars I used to have when I was a kid.

I think I have worked out what Mr Woolley is watching. Jade presses a button on her smart phone, and smirks to herself, and then you can faintly hear the buzz of Aaron's phone vibrating to show that he's received a text message. He reads it, and laughs, and then he presses some buttons on his phone, and so on. Mr Woolley walks between the desks. It looks at first as if he is going to the back of the room to do something with the window. I have never noticed before, but the soles of Mr Woolley's shoes don't make any noise when he walks. A few of the students look curiously at Mr Woolley. They look at him like he is an old, blind Labrador with no collar that had wondered into the college. Jade and Aaron don't notice him at all: they just carry on sending texts to each other.

Mr Woolley grabs the phone out of Jade Kennington's hand. She is taller and probably stronger than Mr Woolley, but he takes her by surprise. He glances at the screen, and his face goes red. His mouth turns down at the corners. He turns his back on the class, and struggles with something. He is doing something with Jade's phone. He pulls the phone's battery out. It slips from his grasp and slides across the floor. He gives the dead phone back to Jade, walks over and picks up the battery, and puts it in his trouser pocket.

'You may collect your battery when the lesson is over,' he says. His voice sounds strange, like he's got a really bad sore throat. Jade is speechless. She looks stunned for a minute, and then she starts laughing. She looks at each of her friends in turn, shrugs, and laughs.

Mr Woolley goes back to the front of the classroom. He rubs the diagram off the whiteboard. He puts all the sheets that he has taken out of the file back in it. He closes the file, turns round, and drops the file in the litter bin. He moves the other file to the centre of the desk, and opens it.

'Alan Mathison Turing was born in London in 1912. He graduated with a degree in mathematics from King's College, Cambridge, in 1934,' says Mr Woolley. Nobody in the class is listening to him, except me. I start writing down the key points in what Mr Woolley is saying: dates, names, important words. 'Turing is regarded as the father of modern computing.' I write that down as well. I can't remember the last time Mr Woolley said the word "father".

Among the class, there are no fights or arguments going on, and nobody is playing music or a loud video game, but they are talking among themselves as if Mr Woolley is not here. For the first time that I can remember, he doesn't seem to mind. He carries on talking in a voice that I can only just hear above the background noise. He talks to the back of the room. He talks to the side of the room. He notices me, and he talks to me. He writes a few points on the whiteboard. When he is not writing on the whiteboard, instead of bouncing back and forth between the whiteboard and the teacher's desk, he walks round to the front of the desk and leans against it, facing me, which is good because it means he is a bit nearer and I can hear more of what he is saying.

'Turing was a fascinating figure. Something of a mysterious figure,' says Mr Woolley. I don't write this down, because it isn't really a fact and I know it already. I know a bit about Alan Turing. I am waiting for Mr Woolley to stop talking for a moment, so I can ask him a question. He talks for a long time about World War Two, and the German Enigma machine, which the Nazis thought could encrypt a message in a way that was unbreakable. He talks about how the code-breakers at Bletchley Park could break the code just by working on paper with their brains, but they needed to do it faster and more efficiently, and so they developed machines to do it. And that is how computers started. 'That's why we are here, in this lesson,' says Mr Woolley. He pauses, and looks round the room. Aaron Braithwaite has put his headphones on and is playing a video game. Jade Kennington, without her smart phone, is sitting and staring into space. Gilbert Owusu is pretending to play drums as he listens to his MP3 player. I want Mr Woolley to get through the parts to do with the war so that I can ask him how Alan Turing died. But Mr Woolley is hardly saying anything. He keeps pausing, and looking round the room. 'What do you think they were fighting for? All those soldiers, sailors, airmen. All those merchant seamen, fighter pilots, bomber crews, tank crews, artillery men. All those factory workers, ARP wardens, home guard, medics, nurses. What do you think they were fighting for?' I can't tell whether he is talking to me or not, even though I am the only person who is listening. 'And why do you think they developed electronic machines, capable of being configured to perform a range of tasks by means of the stored instructions that we now refer to as software?

'I'll tell you why. It was so that Aaron Braithwaite could sit through the entire lesson with his headphones on, playing Call of Duty – something profoundly ironic about that title, here, I can't help thinking. It was so that he and Jade Kennington could sit and play text tennis, and speculate in the most prurient and offensive manner on whether the tutor is what they are pleased to refer to as a "cheese-gobbler". Given that they find the practice of homosexuality so fascinating, it is a pity they cannot be bothered to listen to what I am saying, because Alan Turing was, in fact, a homosexual.' A few of the class stop talking for a moment, glance nervously at Mr Woolley, and then carry on talking. 'He was prosecuted for being a homosexual in 1952. It is believed that MI5 considered him to be a security risk, because of his susceptibility to blackmail. He died in 1954, of cyanide poisoning. We cannot be certain what caused this – '

'Sir?' says Jade Kennington.

'Yes, Jade.'

'Why are you telling us this?'

'Because it's interesting.'

'It isn't interesting at all, Sir. You're just spouting off about some dork we've never heard of.'

'Jade, I am very sorry you feel that way. I am sure somebody in the class finds it interesting. Does anybody find the subject of Alan Turing's contribution to electronic computing, or his mysterious death, interesting?'

'I do, Sir,' I say.

'Thank you, Mason. I was sure I could rely on you.' Somebody says something which I don't quite catch. It might have been, 'He can rely on Mason Bentley to suck him off'. Mr Woolley just carries on talking. 'Whether you regard Alan Turing's career as an interesting subject or not, you cannot deny the impact that his pioneering work has had on our lives. Every time you go on YouTube to watch skateboarding cats, every time you download pornography, or pirated music or videos, every time you go online to buy anything, book anything, check a timetable, or place an underage bet, you are using technology which derives from Turing's work.' It is coming up to the end of the lesson. The other students get ready to leave the classroom, which makes even more noise than when they are talking. They don't wait for Mr Woolley to tell them they can go. They just put their coats on, pick up their bags and leave with a scraping of chair-legs. Jade Kennington goes up to Mr Woolley and asks for her phone battery. He hands it to her. As the class crowds round the door, waiting to get out, I am the only one still sitting and listening. 'And, had it not been for the intelligence obtained from the breaking of the Enigma cipher, this country would now be ruled by Nazis, and we would have no freedom to do any of these things. Every aspect of life, certainly including mobile communication, would be under constant surveillance and control by the state.'

I want him to look at me and carry on talking, but he doesn't. Once the crowd of students has left and the door is clear, Mr Woolley picks up his stuff and leaves. There is no other class waiting to come in, and so I just sit there with my pad and pen on the desk in front of me. I sit there for a long time.

Valves

My name is Alexander Gebb. Refer to me as, "Assistant Gebb" if anyone comes in. I am Assistant 4th Secretary to the Office of Information in District 17 of the Socialist Republic of Suriya. I can see that your documentation is in such a mess that even the Ministry of Internal Affairs could not have produced such a convincing portrayal of a destitute and clueless alien. That means that you are not working for the Ministry of Internal Affairs, and so I can tell you that I have been in post for 15 years and was, until recently, fairly content. Then, a few months ago, things started to get very bad.

Before all this dreadful business began, a typical working day would start at 08:17. Seventeen minutes is the amount of time it takes the valves in the teletype machine in the room next to my office to heat up. In some branches of the Office of Information, they keep the teletype machines on 24 hours a day, to avoid having to let them warm up in the morning, but that costs a lot in electricity and replacement valves, and sometimes requires a machine to be out of commission for days, while it undergoes repairs. Nobody told me directly that I should arrive seventeen minutes before 8 o'clock, so that the machine would be warmed up for when I am officially supposed to start work, and so I wouldn't. I would arrive at eight. I would turn the machine on. While I was waiting, I would either make some coffee, or go to the lavatory and throw up.

How I would spend the morning would depend on whether any messages came in before about nine or nine-thirty. It was even rarer that what came in at that time was of any importance. It was quite common that my hangover was sufficient to merit a return to bed for a couple of hours, which is what I usually did. Fortunately, my apartment is only three stops along the Wudz metro system from the office, and I get an unlimited weekday travel warrant as an employee of the Office of Information. I have a little bunk in one of the unused storerooms in the office, but I prefer to sleep it off at home if possible.

That unlimited weekday travel warrant used to be a major part of my income. Because of an administrative error at the Office of Movement and Logistics, as well as being sent an annual travel warrant, I also received a weekly one as well – every week, of course. I also discovered that, by applying to the Office of Movement and Logistics in different names, I could obtain both another annual travel warrant and another weekly one. Naturally, I would sell the annual warrants to wealthy people who were without the blessing of working for the Suriyan government, and the weekly ones to anyone who wanted one. Many of the buyers in both categories turned out to be prostitutes. That is how I met Karelya. And Larisa. And Zaralya. And Halenya and Rakushya on alternate Tuesdays and Thursdays. But it is Karelya who I fell in love with.

Karelya was impressed when I told her that I worked in District 17. She asked me where I lived. The fact that I failed to answer immediately told her that it was not in District 17.

'District 8?' she asked, as we were putting our clothes back on. District 8 is a mainly residential district, with a nice park and non-state-owned coffee shops, almost as respected as District 17.

'No.'

'District 16?' That is a semi-rural area with a low crime rate but requiring a long journey to one's place of work.

'No.'

'District 7.' It was an accusation.

'Yes.' I knew there was no point in lying to her. Her profession required her to be able to tell on the spot whether a man was telling the truth. I live three metro stops from the office, only one of which is in District 7, and I knew it would count against me with a woman like Karelya. She was looking for a senior party official, or a high-ranking military officer, or the head of a big department or corporation. I knew I had fallen in love with her, and had already resolved to behave like a party boss, or a general, or a fat-cat. I had to make District 7 fit with a persona that might stand a chance of winning Karelya's heart.

'Of course I live in District 7. Where else would you expect me to live?'

'A district where they have nice apartments.'

'I have other apartments. I live in District 7 because that is where I am needed.' I had learnt by that point that Karelya would tend to respond to a single statement by asking two questions. It was quite easy to confuse her by making statements more than one at a time, so that she would lose track of the questions she wanted to ask.

'And why are you needed in District 7?'

'Because that is where things happen. That is the focus of operations.' I finished getting dressed. I put on my overcoat and my leather gloves. I went into the kitchenette of Karelya's District 1 apartment and opened the cupboard under the sink. I found some cleaning-rags and a bottle of 'Purge!' I went back into the bedroom and wiped the bars of the bedstead. I wiped around the wash-basin, and all the doorknobs in the apartment.

'Why are you doing this?' she asked. I didn't answer. We had agreed a price of 200 shintels. I opened my wallet, and counted out 220 shintels.

'It's 200,' she said, as if to say, 'You idiot!' She held out the two extra 10 shintel notes.

'Think of that as a bonus for over-fulfilling your quota.'

She looked at me indulgently, and then kissed me. It was still exquisite, despite the smell of cleaning fluid in the background. I told her I would call her again in ten days or so – which would be after payday and after the next lot of travel warrants – and got out of there as fast as I could. I was wondering what kind of charade I could play out at my next visit in order to maintain an air of mystery. Wiping away imagined fingerprints every time would be inconvenient and likely to wear thin.

Anyway, this blissful arrangement went on for many months, until the recent trouble started.

***

My name is Consul Axel Heinrikke. No further harm will come to you, as long as you co-operate with me. I am the Cephthankyan Consul to the Republic of Suriya. I can see that you are aghast to think that anyone of high Cephthankyan birth would sully himself by dealing with the scum of Suriya, but I can assure you that the job is important, and it does have some compensations.

Coming as I do from a noble Cephthankyan family which survived the revolution, I can say that I have my own interpretation of our party's ideology. Rarely do I rise before 10am, and, on days when I do, I often return to bed for a while after I have settled whatever matters have surfaced. Nearly all of them are trivial. I save important business for the afternoon and evening.

All this, of course, was before the recent crisis.

One of the compensations of being shunted-off to work in Suriya is that the whores in Wudz are reputed to be among the most obliging in the world. I have taken it upon myself, in the national interest of Cephthankya, to catalogue as many of the finer ones as I can, and list all their contacts. A fairly safe bet is a woman called Karelya. She seems to be of superior stock to most other Suriyan women. I wonder if she comes from an aristocratic family. Her couture and appearance bear this out. Her situation is clearly well above the poverty of most Suriyans. Her clothes all seem to be imported, which is most unusual. The Suriyan Socialist Party maintains an iron grip on foreign travel and foreign trade, and so I imagine she has clients who have influence in the government. As soon as I have established who those contacts are and which departments they work in, I will order the foreign branch of the Cephsekpol to abduct her and search her apartment. That will probably be a good time for me to return home. I will have had enough of living in Wudz by then, and more than enough of Suriyan food and the mirthless, grey, buttoned-up rituals and tuneless dirges which pass for Suriyan culture. If it weren't for Karelya, and the fact that my salary is paid in Cephthankyan gold batons which are worth 15 times their face value on the black market, life would be intolerable. I read somewhere that most of the gold content of the batons is mined in Suriya. I hope the gold is properly assayed by Cephthankyan metallurgists before it goes into our coins.

All this is assuming that the crisis does not cause me to have to return to Cephthankya prematurely. I have already started to send some of my furniture and antiques back home in trunks labelled as diplomatic bags. That also helps to prepare the way for Karelya's abduction: many of them are large enough to conceal a body in. I could not of course vouch for the comfort or safety of the journey of one of these bags, even if it had air-holes in it. Heavy sedation would probably be the most humane choice.

I congratulate you heartily on your escape from your cell in the Ministry of Information, but now I have other business to attend to.

***

My name is Gantulga. I like coming here because it never closes, except for an hour after dawn when they clear out the rubbish. I've travelled to Wudz a hundred times in the last few years, and this is still one of the only places in the city I know. What the hell happened to you, by the way? You look like you've been hit by a truck. Oh, I get it. You're another one of those people who have experienced the hospitality of the Suriyan Ministry of the Interior. No, I don't want to know why. I know nothing, and I don't want to know anything. I am a Kyrkylian. Once you become a guest of our Ministry of the Interior, you stay that way forever. There's nothing wrong with you that a few shots of provshk won't fix, even if the stuff in here is like child's piss compared to genuine Kyrkylian spirit.

Why am I not wearing a uniform? I'm a petroleum engineer. I've been working on the construction of a pipeline from Kyrkyl to Suriya. It's a good job. Or it was. It is all about to go to hell. I got a big raise in salary when they told me that I would be working outside Kyrkyl. The project was planned to last 2 years, but I have managed to make my part of it last much longer. The valves for the pipeline are imported from a corporation in Cephthankya, and I found a way of returning a few out of every batch to the manufacturer, on the grounds that they were faulty. This wasn't true of course: Cephthankyan engineering doesn't come cheap, and that's why it's usually well-made. Without valves, the pipe-fitters could not work, which didn't bother them. Some of them got the idea that I was trying to make their lives easier, and started giving me a few kouteks each week out of their wages, by way of encouragement. There was nowhere to spend those, of course, apart from the Kyrkylian Petroleum Institute shop next to the workers' camp. I've been saving them, and so I should be having quite a party when I get home.

Another income from this job has been the payment I get from my contact at the Cephthankyan Valve and Union Corporation. He has found a way of putting the "replacement" valves on top of the production figures for his quota. He receives a bonus, which is paid in Cephthankyan gold batons, a few of which he gave to me. You can buy anything with those. Someone told me that the gold in them comes from the mines in northern Kyrkyl. I saved some of them and the rest I converted into Suriyan shintels. On the black market, you can get 30 times as many shintels in return for gold as you would for the same face value of Cephthankyan paper currency.

So I was doing all right, until it all went to hell. Shall we have another bottle of provshk?

Some of the shintels I spent in a place run by a woman called Karelya. She certainly knows what she's doing. Take that any way you want, but I mean it mostly to do with the way she runs her business. Her place may not be the biggest whorehouse in Wudz, but it must easily be the most profitable. You won't see any soldiers below the rank of colonel in there. Now it seems certain that I will be going back home, I am thinking of making her a proposition. I am going to suggest that she moves her entire establishment to Kyrkyl. That is not as crazy as it sounds. If war does break out, Kyrkyl will come off much better than Suriya. That is as certain as anything in war can be. And her girls would seem more exotic in Kyrkyl than they do here. There will still be generals and diplomats and managers who will require her services – probably more so, if there is a war. With all the contacts she has made in Wudz, there should be no problem about visas or documentation from either the Suriyan or the Kyrkylian government, and my offer to her would be to find a nice place in Commune A1 for her to use – a big, pre-revolution building near all the principal embassies and ministries. I also know people who would keep the local hoodlums, including those from the Ministry of the Interior, at bay.

If she's got as much sense as I think she has, she'll say yes.

***

Ah, it's you again. You seem to be looking better. I come here because it is suitably far from where I work at the Office of Information. Help yourself to a shot of provshk, if you like. I know it is a bit early, but I feel the need of it.

I called Karelya's number. What response did I get?

'Who's speaking?' I put the telephone down immediately. It was a man's voice. A horrible, gruff man who sounded as if he was from the Ministry for Internal Affairs. It was fortunate that I had called from a phone box in a Wudz metro station. I wondered what the hell had happened to Karelya. Even if all her girls had been struck down by plague or influenza, there is no way that she would have allowed a gruff-sounding man to answer the telephone.

I went to the kiosk and picked up a copy of the *Wudz Worker*. I turned to the personal column. There was still an advert for Karelya's. I went back to the phone box and called the number for the Wudz Worker advertising department. I know that all the advertisements placed have to be approved by the Office of Information. That is not my job, but I know the people who do it. I went through the formalities which established that I did not want to place an advertisement, but wished to enquire about one, and so I was put through to the Office of Information. I spoke to three or four dummies and was then connected to 2nd Assistant Plav Grobb, the man I wanted to talk to.

'Is Karelya's place still trading?'

'I can't tell you that.' I knew that that meant 'no'.

'Do you know where Karelya is now?'

'I can't tell you that.' I knew that that meant 'yes'.

'Is she still in Suriya?'

'I can't tell you that.' I knew that that meant 'yes'.

'Is she in a prison camp?'

'No.' I knew that that meant 'yes'.

'Is she in Camp 17B?' That was an educated guess. It has a good railway link from Wudz. Most prisoners from Wudz are sent there, unless they are in a sensitive category.

'Definitely not.'

'Thank you.' At least I know where she is. The life expectancy of a person of sound mind and body in that camp is several years. I can relax, while I think of what to do. Comrade Grobb is often helpful.

***

The Cephsekpol report on the raid on Karelya's premises is infuriating. They were too late. They found the door off its hinges, and all the floorboards taken up. The place was deserted, and everything of value had been taken away. The idiots who carried it out were not even experienced or astute enough to work out whether it was the Surintsec or the Kyrkexburo which had carried out the raid. If you know anything about where Karelya is, it would be greatly in your interest to let us know, immediately. I wonder how whoever it was had time to do such a thorough job, because there were always people going in and out the place – many of them important people.

My relief at not having been there myself while this particular raid happened is more than offset by the embarrassment and inconvenience caused to me by the fact that Karelya's establishment is no longer a going concern. I had taken a great deal of time and trouble to persuade State Commissioner Dagmerk, our minister of foreign affairs, to visit Wudz, with a view not just to seeing if diplomacy could avert the impending crisis, but also to sampling some of the finer cultural experiences of the city, these being limited to Karelya's place and virtually nothing else. I have just about managed to persuade him to return home, as soon as the ostensible purpose of his visit has been carried out. I would much rather he went, rather than try to offer him something else that would fall short of the expectations I allowed myself to raise in his mind, before I was in possession of the facts of the current situation. I expect the State Commissioner and I will be travelling together. There is nothing left for me here and, despite the extraordinary negotiating skills of the State Commissioner, I doubt that war can be prevented. Everyone knows that the Cephthankyan soldier is the best-equipped, most highly-trained and bravest fighting man in the world, and so let us hope that the conflict will be short. I forget where you said you were from, but I advise you to return there yourself, and as soon as possible – after you have told us everything you know about Karelya.

This situation has greatly upset my routine, and that is having a bad effect on my health. I think it must be something the matter with my heart. That is another excellent reason to go back to Cephthankya: one shudders to think what goes on inside Suriyan hospitals. I don't know what they call what they practice here, but no civilised person would refer to it as medicine.

Can you hear that strange whining noise? It sounds almost like an air-raid siren. I think I might go down into the basement, just in case. That'll give me a chance to select a few bottles of Riskkler to decant in time for dinner with the State Commissioner. The '98 was rather good, and I have even got a magnum of the '86 left, which I have been saving for a rainy day. I am sure State Commissioner Dagmerk will appreciate that. As well as being a great statesman and a mighty warrior of the Cephthankyan people, he is known to possess an exceptional palette.

**

102

Hello, again, comrade – and, before you ask, yes, I have been here most of the day and, yes, I am a little bit drunk. I'm leaving tomorrow. That is, in a few hours. Did you hear about the so-called "air-raid" earlier this evening? Stupid load of fuss. Yes, some planes did fly over, but all they were doing was testing the readiness of the Wudz air-defences – and the answer seemed to be, "not at all ready". People are convinced that whole districts have been reduced to rubble, and a few of them seem determined to stay all night in the metro, in case there is another wave, but I know it was just a probing exercise. Stupid, stupid load of fuss. I also know where they came from. I'll tell you a secret. They were Kyrkylian planes. I know. I was an air-cadet when I did my national service. I always got top marks for silhouette recognition of all planes – but on Kyrkylian planes, I was infallible.

I'm getting a train at 4:30. I wouldn't be surprised if that is the last until this war, or whatever it is, is over. Everybody knows that Kyrkyl has the largest air force in the world.

Anyway, I have got a long train journey ahead of me, and so why don't we have another bottle of provshk? Or make that two bottles? I'm sure Vekylya here could do with something to get her in the mood. Anyway, we were talking about Karelya. Vekylya, my darling, I wish you would not try to whisper in my ear while I am talking to this gentleman from overseas. Yes, I know you have things to say, but not now. Yes, I know you want to talk about decadent Western Art, but not now, not here, not while I am talking to Mr... What did you say your name was?

I need to talk to Karelya, to tell her my business proposition. I am sure she will be interested.

***

'So you were not working for the Ministry of Internal Affairs, but I am still chained to this radiator and still naked. Who are you working for? It would be almost worth another two hundred slaps in the face to find out. Are you fucking Karelya? I was going to ask you not to answer that. I see now that you won't.

'I hope you are fucking her, because I want her to be safe.'

103

Pick-up Technique

01:48 26/07/2011
From: beatrice_hottie@blueyonder.co.uk
To: annabelfromhell@talktalk.net

'Wuthering Heights'

My dearest, darling Annabel:

I am trying to decide between a sleeping pill or another page of the book which you recommended to me so persuasively. I am not being sarcastic when I say that I am grateful to you, because I get very hyper when I am revising for exams, particularly this maths scholarship, and sometimes I go the whole night just reading textbooks and exam papers and never closing my eyes once. I took a break and picked up 'Wuthering Heights'. I must admit that I found it instantly soporific. I think all the exciting bits you described so powerfully must be later on. But I will persevere with it, I promise. If you recommended me to read the phone book, I would definitely give it a go, my darling.

Since the party last week, I have also found a use for the digital photograph frame that somebody gave me for Christmas. I have transferred all the pictures I took of you, especially the ones outside on the terrace when we were alone together. I watch them in 'slideshow' mode while I am waiting to go to sleep.

I can't wait to see you again. Is Devlin having another party soon? I would ask to come to your house, but I remember your saying how difficult things are in parentville at the moment. You could always come here of course, if you could tolerate my dysfunctional family. I don't care where we meet, as long as it's soon.

I am going to lie down and look at the pictures of you again, now. I hope I have a deliriously beautiful message from you tomorrow.

Good night, my darling Annabel. XXXXXXX

23:56 01/08/2011
From: annabelfromhell@talktalk.net
To: beatrice_hottie@blueyonder.co.uk

greetings from putney

my dearest bea , i have moved in to the flat at long last. it took all day , Calina was an absolute treasure as usual. she just had a russian football shirt and denim shorts on and she got me almost as hot and bothered as she was after she had shifted a few boxes up those awful stairs. i was tempted i can tell you , but i was good for once. anyway i cannot tell you how much of a relief it is to be away from those bastard parents of mine. daddy gave me 500 squids - some kind of weird "leaving present" i suppose. she who thinks she must be obeyed was tearful and they had some kind of vulgar row just as i was getting my cases together. guess what – i took the opportunity to tiptoe down to the cellar and grab a couple of bottles of mumm. they clinked together in my bag as i was getting into the car but nobody noticed. i stopped off at devlins powder emporium and parted with some of the 500 squids. ill save some for you , i promise. anyway , cheers sweetie. nightie night. sleep tight. xxxXXXxxx

ps brrrrrr it is as cold as siberia in this flat but ill survive. wish you were here to keep me warm and snug xx

00:11 02/08/2011
From: beatrice_hottie@blueyonder.co.uk
To: annabelfromhell@talktalk.net

привет киса[1]

My Dearest, Most Precious Annabel:

So sorry to hear of your ordeal in the frozen wastes. Maybe the arctic climate will cool your ardour for the devoted serf, Calina. I trust you didn't catch anything – like potato blight or Colorado beetles – off her. I hope you don't feel lonely in your new surroundings. I was looking at my exam calendar this morning (please do try to stay awake – I'm not going to give you a lecture on the binomial theorem) and it struck me that, three days ago, it was exactly one year since we first got to know each other. I think I have learnt more from being with you than I did in the previous 16 years.

I ought to go to sleep now because I have a scholarship exam in the morning but it's only algebra analysis and so I don't need to revise. My folks are being so middle class about my getting into an American university. I would actually be quite excited about it except that you still have not said definitely that you will come to Boston with me if I get in.

Good night, my darling Annabel. XXXXXXX

6 Aug 2011 15:06

Hi bea , great news about your scholarship. have had a

rocketing idea for what we can do to celebrate before

you go to amerikay. ill email you tonight. when do you

think you can come round to the flat? miss you xxxx

---

[1] Hello pussycat

6 Aug 2011 15:09

Thought you would never ask. Can't tonight. Mum's taken
me shopping in London and to see a show as a good
conduct prize but will get away tomorrow without fail.
Can't wait to read your email. Miss you, too. XXXXXX

01:19 07/08/2011
From: annabelfromhell@talktalk.net
To: beatrice_hottie@blueyonder.co.uk

rules of the game

my dearest bea , here is the game i said we would have. if i
win, you have to give me those vivienne westwood shoes
your mama bought for you for passing your exams. if you win
(not that you have a chance ha ha) then i promise you a night
to remember at my flat, just the two of us, and breakfast in
bed.

your mission should you choose to accept it is first to steal a
car.

when i say "car" i dont mean any old jalopy , i mean
something expensive and sexy. dont panic. i have called in a
favour with devlin (let;s say i;m cashing in my loyalty card
points ha ha) and he can get you some very passable
documents if you want to do it by taking one for a test drive
from a dealership. i know they usually insist on sending some
stripey-shirted salesman out with you but you could say
you;ve been felt up before or something and that you want to
go on your own. i am sure you can convince them. your
hardest job will probably be to get them to give you the keys
to something with a proper-sized engine and not some girlie
runaround.

when you have got the wheels you must go to the airport.
come to think of it , which airport?? doesn't matter. you can
go to any airport you like but you must pick someone up ,
male or female but it must be an adult , not a child , and not
anybody disabled or blind or anything. they have to be
compos thingummy. you have to get them into the car and
keep them there for one hour. take a digital camera and snap
a photo of them when they get in and then again after the

107

hour is up and the times shown on the pictures will prove you have done it. then split and get back to my flat asap. ive posted you a key. yes my darling , your very own key to my flat to keep forever and ever and ever (or at least until the lease expires). last one back is a sissy. oh and you are not allowed to get run in. if the rozzers get you then you;re out.

are you in???

*

Hello, my name is Eamon Brown. Good morning. It is still morning, isn't it? My name is Eamon Brown. Thank you for inviting me. Pleased to meet you. My name is Breamon Own – Eamon Brown. My name is –

There is someone here to meet me. That's weird. I am sure the letter didn't mention anything about being picked up at the airport. The sign is pretty clear: MR BROWN FROM LEEDS. That's me, all right. My god, that lass is attractive. She does look a bit overdressed though, especially in those shades. I wonder if they're real Ray-Bans.

'Hello. My name is Eamon Brown.'

'Follow me, please.'

'I think the plane landed a few minutes early.'

'Whatever.'

'Pardon?'

'Nothing. Nothing at all. The car's over there.'

'That's a very nice car. I don't think I've driven in a 7-series before. My dad used to have a 5-series, but it was years old.'

'Well it has four wheels, so that's a start. It's stolen.'

'Ha! Ha! Ha! Ha! Classic. I didn't know you were allowed to park this close to the terminal.'

'You aren't.'

'Oh. Is it far?'

'Is what far?'

'To the interview.'

'Oh, that. Yes, quite far. It'll take about an hour.'

'What, with the traffic and everything?'

'It'll take an hour.'

'Why are you taking a picture of me?'

'I need a time-stamped picture of you.'

'Why do you need that?'

'I'll tell you later.'

'Is it a security thing? Or performance management, or something?'

'I'll tell you later.'

*

'Ah, the open road. Do you like the open road, Mr Brown?'

'Er, yes. I suppose so. Is it, er...'

'What? Come on, don't be shy.'

'Is it really necessary to drive this fast? You must be doing over a hundred.'

'I always drive at over a hundred miles an hour whenever possible.'

'Er, I see. Why is that, if you don't mind me asking? And you said you were going to tell me why you took that photograph of me.'

'WANKER! Sorry, Mr Brown, not you – the bald tosser in the Mercedes. Though I expect you probably are a wanker as well, by the look of you. Are you a wanker?'

'Er...'

'Never mind. I am only trying to make conversation, and I must admit that you look particularly boring. Ether in human form, I thought, as soon as I saw you.'

'That's not a very nice thing to say. Is this some kind of psychometric evaluation?'

'What are you talking about?'

'Is that why you're so nasty and sarcastic? Is it some kind of pre-interview test? Why can't you just be nice?'

'I don't do nice. I am not a nice person. I hate nice. Nice sucks. Nice is for people like you.'

'Well I think it's unprofessional. People like me? What do you mean, "people like me"?'

'Losers. Little people. People who attend former polytechnics. Did you attend a former polytechnic?'

'I have just graduated from Leeds Metropolitan University. I got a first.'

'What did I tell you? And you read – don't tell me, don't tell me – I bet it was Business Studies: something to fall back on when the pub band you are a member of turns out to be a non-starter.'

'Business Information Systems. And I'm not in a band. Where did you go to university?'

'Going. I'm only seventeen. I'm going to MIT next year. And I don't have a driving licence, by the way.'

'Why would Global Consulting Corporation send somebody without a driving licence to pick me up from the airport?'

'It should be obvious to you that I am nothing to do with Global Consulting Corporation.'

'Then why did you pick me up at the airport?'

'For a bet. My friend Annabel and I are having a competition in which we each have to steal a car, pick up a random person from the airport, and keep them moving for one hour. The first one back to Annabel's flat with the evidence is the winner.'

'I am going to be late for my interview. This is kidnap. This is against the law.'

'Most of what I do is against the law. But think of it as though I am doing you a favour. If we live through the next few hours, I promise you that the rest of your life will not be the same, Mr Brown.'

'I hate being late. I've got to get to my interview. It's vitally important. This job is going to be my big break.'

'Not any more. Soz.'

' "Soz". Is that all you've got to say? "SOZ"?'

'Don't be such a spoilsport. You're making me very, very bored. If I fall asleep, I'll crash the car.'

'At least we are heading in vaguely the right direction. The interview is on Fenchurch Street.'

'I'll make a note not to go anywhere near Fenchurch Street.'

'Why can't you just drop me off there?'

'Read my lips, Mr Brown: you are not going to that interview.'

'Why not? I don't understand. And for goodness' sake, will you SLOW DOWN?'

'Who are you texting?'

'It's none of your business.'

'I hope it isn't anything to do with your precious bloody interview. I'll have that, thank you.'

'HEY! Give that back!'

'Whee! There it goes. Straight out onto the A23.'

'That was my mobile. That was my personal mobile.'

'Aww. Diddums. Ha! Ha! You're not actually crying, are you? Oh, this is priceless. I bet I'm doing miles better than Annabel.'

'Why do you keep taking pictures of me?'

'I'm going to send it to Annabel. You look even more pathetic when you cry than you do normally.'

'You're going to have to slow down if you insist on texting someone while you're driving.'

*

15 Aug 2011 11:09

Mine is called Mr Brown – most interesting thing about

him. How's yours? x

15 Aug 2011 11:17

business man from ruislip. he seems to think im going to

get messy with him. i will do no such thing. youre a few

minutes ahead of me you fiend.

15 Aug 2011 11:23

Look! He's crying. Lip started to tremble when I threw

his phone out of the car. x

15 Aug 2011 11:28

you cruel hardcore bitch ha ha ha.

15 Aug 2011 12:03

driving to yr flat now. cant wait to claim prize

*

'Can I borrow your mobile, since you destroyed mine?'

'No.'

'Will you SLOW DOWN?'

'No. Actually, yes. We're stopping, now. We're here. I'll just get the second photograph. That's it. Bye.'

'Where's "here"?'

'Annabel's flat: the finishing line.'

'Don't you know how to park?'

'I don't need to park. We just need to ditch. I don't need it anymore. I don't need you anymore.'

'I need to borrow a phone. Hey! I need to borrow a phone.'

'Will you stop following me?'

'Does the flat have a phone? '

'I'm not telling you: you can't come in.'

'I've got to get to a phone.'

'Use a phone box.'

'Where is there one?'

'Just get lost, will you.'

'Which house is it?'

'LET GO OF ME.'

'My name is Eamon Brown. I play hooker for Dewsbury Rams, and I am not letting go of you until you tell me which flat you are going to and let me use the phone.'

'You're hurting me.'

*

'My throat's really sore, now.'

'I told you it was a waste of time expecting anybody in London to take any notice when you scream "Let me go! Let me go!" Do you live in this flat, as well?'

'No. Annabel lives here on her own.'

'How come you've got a key, then?'

'We're friends – not that it's any of your business. The phone's on the wall in the kitchen, through there. Do not, under any circumstances, touch anything other than the phone – and be as quick as you can.'

*

15 Aug 2011 12:09

Annabel, where are you? I have phoned you three times now but I just get voicemail. What's happening? Anyway I have won the bet hands down, haven't I?. It is tonight, isn't it, The Night To Remember? XXX

'I got through to GCC. They were OK about it. In fact, the person I spoke to seemed to think it was quite funny. The interview's been re-scheduled. And they said I could claim hotel expenses for tonight.

'I could do with a cup of tea, actually. I've put the kettle on. Do you want one?'

'No, I don't.'

'Please yourself. This Annabel –'

'Yes – what about Annabel? Why are you bothering me with questions about Annabel? What do you want to know concerning Annabel? I suppose you are going to ask me where she is. Well, I don't know. I have texted her and phoned her but it went through to voicemail. I expect she is on her way here. Maybe she thinks she still has a chance of winning the bet.'

'Er, no. It was nothing to do with where she is. I was just wondering if you knew whether she was interested in rugby.'

'In rugby. Do you mean the awful game, played by horrible men – that kind of rugby?'

'And women. Yes. Rugby league, I mean, rather than union.'

'Are you out of your tiny, microscopic mind? Why the hell are you asking me whether Annabel is interested in your loathsome, barbaric, working-class excuse to have a fight in the mud?'

'I collect rugby shirts, and there's one I happened to notice on the floor of the bedroom which is rather unusual. Do you think she would sell it to me?'

'First of all, you had no business even to glance into the bedroom. That bedroom is a private and sacred space. And secondly, I refuse to believe that what you think you saw is a rugby shirt.'

'Have a look if you don't believe me. It's the blue one with white side-panels. It's got letters of the Russian alphabet on it. It's for a team called Moscow Storm. The head coach used to play for –'

'Can you just remind me why you are still here?'

'It's very rare. You can't order them on the internet – well, not reliably. You did say that Annabel was on her way.'

'Yes, she is.'

'And you don't seem to think that she has much of an interest in rugby?'

'Absolutely nil.'

'Great. That means that she might part with it. You wouldn't mind keeping quiet about how rare I said it was, would you? I was going to offer her thirty-five quid for it. Does she go to the Russian Federation a lot on business, or something?'

'No, I don't think she has ever been to Russia. Tuscany is more Annabel's kind of place, or the south of France.'

'I wonder how she came by it, then. Is Annabel quite a big lass?'

'Annabel is not any sort of "lass". Annabel is a woman. She is a size 8, and so, no, she is not big. She is petite, in fact, like me.'
'Well that shirt must look ridiculous on her. It'd be big on me.'

*

15 Aug 2011 12:49

Annabel: please just let me know where you are. Have you had an accident? I'm really worried now. If you're driving, make SURE you stop safely before replying.

XXX

15 Aug 2011 13:07

hi hun , soz for not picking up b4. v v busy. talk later bye

xx

15 Aug 2011 13:08

Busy with what? Where? With whom? How long for?
What about tonight?

15 Aug 2011 13:16

daddy thinks he has found me a job , he wanted to talk to me about my allowance and to the job ppl. v v important . read a bit more of wuthering heights if youre bored xx

15 Aug 2011 13:17

What about the bet?

15 Aug 2011 13:25

oh that yes. soz do you mean you actually went ahead with it??? xx

15 Aug 2011 13:26

Do you mean that you did not? What about the business man from Ruislip who wanted to get messy?

15 Aug 2011 13:32
no no , i just made that up. i thought you were making it
up 2 sweetie xx

*

'Are you all right?'

'Annabel isn't coming. Annabel's gone.'

'Oh. I wanted to put an offer in for that rugby shirt. Er…I know this might sound daft, but, you know what you said earlier about always breaking the law?'

'What about it?'

'Do you want to do something else that's illegal? Illegal for you, I mean: not for me.'

'What? What are you talking about?'

'Do you fancy going for a quick pint somewhere?'

Submarine Dreams

1977

My brother is still known to me and himself, and not just to our parents, as David. He has, or will have, three obsessions in his life, one after the other: model trains, reggae, and disappearing. The first is carried out mainly inside our parents' house. The second, which has not started yet, both inside and outside our parents' house. The third one will of course take place entirely outside our parents' house.

David is nearly eleven. I am nine. It is the start of the summer holiday. It is morning. David and I are sitting at the breakfast table with Natalie and John. As we eat our cereal and our boiled eggs, John announces to David that today the two of them will begin a summer holiday project together. John says they are going to build a model railway in David's bedroom. David starts bouncing up and down in his chair.

'David, sit still, please,' says Natalie. 'David, sit still, please. David – '

'Oh, let him get excited if he wants to,' says John.

'What gauge / wha-at ga-auge / wha-at ga-auge...' chants David, in what I recognise is the rhythm of the theme music from *Mission Impossible*. Natalie does that thing in which she heaves her shoulders, turns her face upwards, tilts her head to one side, and rolls her eyes to express disapproval. John is happy for David to carry on, and so there is nothing she can do. She starts to clear things off the table and carry them over to the dishwasher. We are in the dining area of the kitchen, not the dining room. I have not quite finished my egg, but Natalie takes it away anyway. I am just about to complain, when she drops the shell into a cup with the dregs of some tea in the bottom of it.

'Please may I leave the table?' I ask Natalie.

'Ye-es,' she sighs, as if to say, 'Yes, if you really must,' which is silly, because she herself has made it clear that the meal is over. I carry the tea pot, the toast rack and some of the plates over to the dishwasher, taking care not to get in Natalie's way. I empty the tealeaves into the compost bin and rinse out the pot, because being told off for not helping would result in something much longer and more boring than

116

clearing the table. I go into the playroom to get my small notebook and a pencil, and then slip out of the kitchen door when Natalie is not looking.

The door of the garage is open. John and David are in John's workshop, measuring pieces of wood. John is showing David how to use a plane. Actually, John is showing John how to use a plane, and David just happens to be nearby. I kick a small stone at the wheel of the camper van. It bounces off the hub-cap with a metallic sound, but they do not even look up. I open the gate and go into the back garden.

Our back garden is about the only part of where we live where you can get any peace. There is a large patio, covered in coloured flagstones and with steps down to the lawn. The lawn is large and square and mowed into stripes by John, who also saturates it in chemicals to kill weeds. If you ate any of the clippings, you would probably die from poison. Next to the lawn is the vegetable garden, the fruit enclosure, the shed and the greenhouse. By the side of the shed is the garage, which is also John's workshop, and where John and David are now. In the west corner, furthest from the house, is the hive for John's bees. I have been stung seven times, two of them at the same time. It is now 238 days since I was last stung, which is a record. David was stung last Saturday. Natalie and John had gone out early, for the whole day. David got out of bed at ten o'clock and went for a walk in the garden in his pyjamas and bare feet. He was doing a kind of ballet dance on the grass when his foot landed on a bee, which immediately stung him. I was watching through the playroom window. The window was open and I could hear him exclaim, 'Oh, what a lovely – aaaaaaarrrgggggh!' I laughed so much that I had to go and hide in the downstairs toilet. I nearly wet my knickers. In the east corner is the old sandpit, from which most of the sand has disappeared. Next to the sandpit is a thing made out of wood and Perspex, with two seats in it, and a toy control panel made out of bits from old electrical appliances and a broken speedometer off one of John's bikes. We used to pretend it was an aeroplane, a spaceship, or a submarine, but David hardly ever likes to play in it any more.

The submarine game was my favourite. David used to wear a black false beard and a peaked cap from the dressing-up box, and talk in a German accent. We used to fire torpedoes at British corvettes and destroyers, and merchant ships. I had to call him 'Herr Kapitän' and do everything he said. Once, he brought us to the surface just after we had sunk a neutral oil tanker heading for England, and he made me open up with the deck gun to set the oil on fire and kill all the crewmen. I didn't want to do it, but he told me I would be court-martialled and shot if I didn't obey orders. Even after I had done it, he tied my hands behind my back and locked me in the brig (the shed) as punishment for insubordination. It got very close to time for dinner, and Natalie was calling me. I think David had forgotten all about the game. Natalie asked him if he knew where I was, and then he remembered. When Natalie started to get annoyed with him for locking me in the shed, he explained that it was part of a game, and he had had to do it because I was an insubordinate member of the Kriegsmarine. She decided not to tell him off after that. David let me out, and untied me before Natalie saw me. Before sitting down for dinner, I pulled the sleeves of my cardigan down to hide the marks that the twine had made.

I check through the dining room windows and the playroom window to make sure that Natalie is not watching me. I take out my notebook and do some more work on The Plan. I am drawing a diagram of the house and garden. I am drawing it on a sheet of A3 paper which I keep folded up in the pocket at the back of my big notebook, but I take the measurements and draw detailed sketches in my small notebook, for adding later. I am measuring the length of the west wall, the one between us and the Goldbergs. I start at the far end from the house, so that I am walking away from the beehive, not towards it, while I go heel-to-toe in a straight line, parallel with the wall, and as close to it as I can manage without overbalancing. I hold onto the privet hedge with my left hand to keep myself steady. I count 145 and a half foot-lengths. I have previously measured the length of my feet in these pumps. My left foot is 218 millimetres, and my right is 220 millimetres, for an average of 219 millimetres. The foot I was putting down when it was just a half, at the end, was my longer, right foot, but the approximation of "a half" makes the difference in length insignificant.

I walk round the garden for a bit longer and take some more measurements. When I go up to my bedroom to modify The Plan, I can hear David and John talking in David's bedroom, and banging and dragging stuff about as they clear the way for the model railway. John has started making a list of things they need to buy. They will be going out soon, probably in the Caravette rather than the Golf, because some of the things they will get might be big. I hope Natalie has got some marking to do, or a seminar to write, or something, because otherwise she will make me go shopping with her, or off on one of her trips which seem to last forever. Last time, she took me to York Minster. It took hours to get there, and when we eventually did get there, she made me do brass rubbing. There were a lot of other people there. They all seemed to have spectacles and greasy hair and sticky-out teeth. It was embarrassing, and terminally boring. I wonder if I can make Natalie believe that The Plan is something to do with a lesson at school. She'd let me work on it as long as I like, then.

I hope David and John go out, soon. All this noise is driving me crazy. Now I can hear David jumping down the stairs, four at a time, in the way that makes Natalie tell him off every time he does it. John is saying something long and complicated about AC transformers. I think they must be just about to leave.

I go into David's bedroom, in which nearly everything has been moved or rearranged. David's bed used to be in the corner, opposite the door, but they have moved it next to the door. All his toy boxes have been moved next to the wardrobe. They have cleared more than half the room for the space where they are going to build the model railway. I wish I had this room: it is about one third larger than mine. I open David's wardrobe and have a look to see if John has rearranged anything in here. It looks as if he has not. The drawers inside have labels on them, written by Natalie with a black marker pen on sticky paper. The top drawer is labelled SOCKS. It contains one pair of socks, four odd socks, and some Lego. The second drawer is labelled T-SHIRTS. It contains underpants, some pieces of a jigsaw with a picture of a steam train on it, and a roll of green insulating tape. The third drawer is labelled UNDERPANTS, and contains nothing but a playing card (the nine of spades). The fourth drawer is labelled SHIRTS, and that is what it contains. Most of David's clean clothes are in a pile at the bottom of the wardrobe, all mixed up.

Underneath the pile of clothes is a carpet. It is the same grey carpet that covers the rest of the floor, but David cut three slits in it with John's craft knife to make a flap which you can lift up. He removed a section of the carpet underlay so that he could put something under

119

the carpet without it making a bulge. The section he removed is slightly larger than a sheet of A4 paper. This is where he keeps Mayfair. He got it from a boy in his year at school called Stephen Westcott. David showed it to me once, but only for a minute. This is the first time I have looked at Mayfair on my own.

I am going to look at every page, so that I will have seen every page at least once. I wish I could take a long time looking at each page, and decide which are my favourite ones, but that will have to wait until Natalie is out of the house as well as John. I wonder how old I will have to get before Natalie and John will leave me in the house on my own, without David.

I don't understand why they put so much writing in this magazine, when they could put more pictures. And I don't understand why they put pictures of things that aren't nudies. All people who look at the magazine want to see is nudies, but that only takes up about half of it.

I get to a lady who is called Danni. She has blonde, curly hair and is quite sun-tanned. She is quite tall: taller than John and Natalie. She is wearing white stockings and suspenders and white shoes. She has a white bra and knickers on in the pictures on the first page, and a long, see-through white skirt, but she takes these off and you can see her nipples and her bottom and her pubic hair. Her pubic hair is blonde and curly, too. I wish I were called Danni. I wish I were Danni. I am going to call myself Danni from now on.

I can hear Natalie shouting for me. I hope she doesn't want to go out. I put Mayfair back under the carpet flap, and I ignore Natalie while I make sure that the flap is properly in place. I put David's messy pile of clothes back over the top of it.

Natalie shouts for me over and over again. SARAH! SARAH! SARAH, WHERE ARE YOU? My name is Danni. I am Danni.

1980

David won't listen to me anymore if I call him David. I am sitting on his bed. School has started again, but it is Saturday. Natalie and John are getting ready for a dinner party at our house this evening. They have gone out to buy things. Natalie started cooking yesterday. David is painting some OO/HO scale plastic figures, which he is going to add to his model railway. He is going to create what he calls a "scene" and I call a "diorama". He is using enamel paint, thinned with white spirit, which he also uses to clean his brushes, when he remembers. Natalie always calls it "turps" and John calls it "turpentine", which is made from the destructive distillation of pinewood, but the stuff that David is using is synthetic white spirit. The white spirit isn't white: it is colourless, and it smells. David is allowed to paint in his bedroom. Natalie won't let us bring drinks or food upstairs − not even a plate with one digestive biscuit on it − but you can bring enamel paint and white spirit. At least, John says that David can. Every time Natalie sees me doing anything in my bedroom except reading, homework, or sleeping, she tells me to take it downstairs and do it in the playroom.

I have not got anything to do at the moment, and so I sit and read the instructions on the box that David's plastic figures came in. He has failed to ensure that the surfaces are grease-free by washing the figures in warm water and detergent, and then allowing to dry thoroughly before painting. David is singing along to a record he is playing. It is a 45 rpm seven-inch single and the A-side is called *Mirror In The Bathroom*, by a band called *The Beat*. This is David's favourite song at the moment. He has started to get into trouble for spending all his pocket money on records. It is since he started buying *2 Tone* records that he insists I call him "Walt Jabsco", or "Walt", which is the name given to the man in the picture in the middle of the records. David does not look anything like the man on the record, but he still insists that his name is Walt Jabsco. In return, Walt has agreed to call me Danni. I must stop thinking about Mayfair Danni. It is ages since I last looked at her pictures. Not thinking about her is really difficult. I wish I could think of something that I want to think about more than I want to think about Mayfair Danni, but I can't.

Walt is waiting for some of the paint to dry, and plays with his model railway. He turns the dial on one of the transformers, presses the switch that controls the direction that the train moves in, and brings the locomotive out of the shed. He stops it at the platform, and attaches some rolling stock. It is one of Walt's "mad" trains: the locomotive, a coal wagon, two Pullman passenger cars, an oil tank, a goods wagon that says, "Palethorpe's Sausages" on the side, a goods wagon that says "Hovis" on the side, a truck with a crane on it, and a truck with a howitzer on it. When I asked him why he didn't use another locomotive and have goods in one train and passengers in another, he said, 'I've put together all the things that the people might need on their journey.' I see. After they have set off from the station, the passengers make the world's largest sausage sandwich on brown bread, which they cook over oil stoves and lift with a crane, and then they fire a salute with the howitzer to celebrate how delicious it was. I suppose the howitzer would also come in handy if they thought an enemy was going to come and try to steal the sandwich, but they would need a lot of data about the enemy's position for the howitzer to be any use.

David is making up his own words to *Mirror In The Bathroom*:

'Mirror in the bathroom please talk free / The door is locked just you and me / Can I take you to a restaurant that's got green tables / You can pick your nose while you are eating.' I much prefer the proper words. Neither of us has the foggiest idea what the song is about, other than something to do with a mirror in the bathroom. I don't get why a mirror would make somebody "drift gently into mental illness", not even if they did that thing with two mirrors opposite each other, which gives you a theoretically infinite number of reflections. And the song only mentions one mirror. Since it says to the mirror "please talk free", it may be the person singing is mad in the first place.

I'm sick of this. I am going back to my room. I have borrowed a book from the library about how to draw figures. I am trying to learn to draw properly so I can draw Mayfair Danni, partly so that I won't have to risk coming into David's room to get Mayfair, and partly because I want to see what Mayfair Danni would look like in different outfits and different positions. I wonder what Mayfair Danni is doing today. She is twenty-two years old. I expect she is doing a postgraduate degree, unless she took some time to go travelling and is now in her final year. She doesn't look like a lawyer or a physicist or a medic. I bet she does something like archaeology, or theology, or fine art. I wonder when her next photo shoot is. I bet she gets paid a lot of money for appearing nude. I bet she does it to pay her fees and rent and things. Her grant is probably quite small.

Oh, god – that's Natalie and John coming back. I can hear Natalie shouting for Sarah. I had better go and see what she wants.

'Who's coming tonight?' I ask as I am emptying and refilling the dishwasher. Natalie must have used every last thing we have in the kitchen except the toast rack and the teapot, which are still clean from after breakfast. She is making Madeira sauce. This is the first time she has tried to make it.

'The Rosewalls, of course,' says Natalie. She has not yet mentioned to me who is coming, and the Rosewalls have never been to our house for dinner before. The only time any of them have been here is when Arthur Rosewall sometimes comes to play with Walt, and Arthur's mother or father comes to pick him up when it is time for him to go home. The Rosewalls have a Caravette, a bit like ours, except theirs is covered in rust and the exhaust makes a funny kind of chugging noise. That's the only car the Rosewalls have got. They use it to pick Arthur up from school.

'Is Arthur coming with them?' I ask. Natalie looks surprised.

'No. Yes. No. I'm not sure.' She dashes out of the kitchen into the hall, where the downstairs telephone is. I can hear her talking to Mrs Rosewall.

'Of course, Marjorie. Yes, of course we assumed he was coming. I just wanted to make sure. And David is looking forward to seeing him. Yes. See you about seven. Yes. Of course. No problem at all. Goodbye.' She puts the phone down. 'Shit,' she says, very quietly, but with emphasis on the letter t, and I hear her quite clearly. She comes back into the kitchen and looks at the clock.

'Sarah?' It sounds like she is going to try to be nice to me. 'Would you want the same food as the grown-ups this evening, or something different?'

'What are the grown-ups having?'

'Vichyssoise…'

'You mean "leek and potato soup".'

'…followed by boeuf en croute, with dauphinoise potatoes, Madeira sauce, and endive and tomato salad, and black cherry and kirsch pavlova for dessert.' The boeuf en croute will have that yucky pate de foie gras between the meat and the pastry. The meat's nice, and the pastry's yummy, but the pate is disgusting. It's the stuff that's made by shoving a pipe with a funnel on the end down a goose's throat and force-feeding it, and it tastes of metal. Dauphinoise potatoes has cream in it, and if you put it on the same plate with meat, it mixes with the meat-juice and makes you feel sick.

'I'll have soup and meringue, but I don't want any main course, except salad and bread and butter.' She sighs with relief. She doesn't want me to know what a big favour I've done her, but she can't help herself. Now she knows she can give my portion of the main course to Arthur.

While Natalie is still thinking about the dinner party, I go out and get on my bike. It is a boy's racer with five gears. It used to belong to David, but John gave it to me when David got his new one, which has ten gears. It is miles better than my old bike. My old one had a low cross-bar, eighteen-inch wheels, only three gears, and a basket on the front. It was a girl's bike. This one is miles faster. I don't go anywhere in particular this time. I just cycle round the block for a while. I think about Mayfair Danni, and I think about Arthur Rosewall. I wonder if David and Arthur are going to let me join in with whatever they decide to do, or if they are going to do what they usually do, and ignore me.

When I get back, Natalie is in a total panic. She is so busy with her cooking, she forgets to tell me to polish the glasses and cutlery and lay the table, and so I do it anyway. Doing something seems easier and less boring if I do it without Natalie telling me to do it. Natalie hears me moving around in the dining room, and comes in, probably to ask me what I am doing. She sees the table, forgets what she was going to say, looks relieved again, and then looks cross.

'Where are the napkins? You've forgotten the napkins!' There's no pleasing some people. The napkins are in the drawer. I have counted them and I was going to do them last.

The Rosewalls arrive at three minutes past seven. Natalie isn't ready. John came back from wherever he went after the shopping trip and has just finished shaving and getting ready. Natalie wanted to tell him to hurry up, but she wasn't brave enough. She had to take it out on David, instead, who didn't seem to understand that it was a proper dinner party and not just an evening visit, and so after his bath, which took ages as usual, he put the same clothes back on that he had been wearing before. Natalie shouted at him and told him to iron a shirt and put some different trousers on. I've got to wear a dress. Natalie ended up having to iron the shirt herself, because David is useless at ironing. He doesn't seem to understand that the idea is to smooth the creases out of the material, not iron more creases in.

Natalie is stressed because we are short of mixers, and she has not had time to go out and buy them, and John didn't get any when he went off on his own.

'Do mixers have alcohol in them?'

'No,' she says, in that exasperated voice she uses when she thinks I'm being stupid. 'You add the mixers to the alcohol. That is why they are called mixers.'

'So I could legally buy them, if you gave me the money.'

'What a stupid suggestion! How would you get to the shop?'

'On my bike. I've got a pannier. I could carry the mixers in my pannier.'

'Er. It isn't very polite to the Rosewalls to go beetling off as soon as they've arrived.'

'None of them want to talk to me, anyway. I don't think they'll notice.'

'Oh, all right then.' She sounds as if she is the one doing me a favour.

I take the stupid dress off and put my jeans, jumper and trainers back on. Natalie gives me a five-pound note, and tells me to get tonic water, soda water and ginger ale, and to bring the change back.

'I'll just go into the sitting room and tell the Rosewalls that I am going out for a little while.'

'Oh. All right. Yes, do that. And apologise. And tell them that you won't be long.'

The door of the sitting room is open. I crawl in on my hands and knees, and nobody notices me. John, Mr and Mrs Rosewall and Arthur are all at the other end of the room, by John's hi-fi. He is showing them a record and giving them a talk about it, something about Wagner. The carpet and underlay absorb any noise. I crawl round the back of the sofa, round the far side, and I can see Marjorie Rosewall's handbag. It is enormous and the zip is unfastened. I dip my hand inside. I feel for her keys, find them, pull them out gently, and crawl out again. Again, nobody notices me. I put the keys in my coat pocket, and get on my bike. I turn my lamps on, and cycle away. It is starting to rain. I had better go to Lockwood's first, before it closes, and get the mixers.

Fortunately, there are no other customers in Lockwood's, and so I get served quickly. After I have put the bottles in my pannier, I cycle as fast as I can to the Rosewall's house, which is not very far from Lockwood's. I know which house it is because I have been in the car when John was giving David a lift there so that he could play with Arthur. And I have seen the address written down in David's very untidy address book. I wrote Arthur's address down in my address book, under R for Rosewall.

I cycle up the Rosewall's drive and straight round to the back of their house. There are no lights on outside. There is a light on somewhere inside the house, but they just left that on to keep burglars away. I've got a torch in my coat pocket. I tested the batteries before I came out. The Rosewall's don't have a burglar alarm. At least, there's no box outside which says they have. I try some of Marjorie's keys in the back door. It has two locks, like ours, a mortise and a Yale, and it opens. It leads into their kitchen.

I go inside, and go straight upstairs. I open the first door I come to, and it is Mr and Mrs Rosewall's bedroom. I have a look in the drawers beside their bed. Apart from books and tissues and pairs of spectacles and headache pills, all I find is a vibrator. I go out and look for Arthur's bedroom. I have a look under his bed, under his mattress, and in his wardrobe. I don't find anything. I can't do a proper search of the whole room with just a little torch, and I don't want to risk switching the light on. I go back into Arthur's parents' bedroom.

There must be something here. I move the torch slowly over the whole room. There's a dressing table. In one of the drawers of the dressing table is a pack of miniature playing cards with pictures of bare-breasted women on them, but that is not what I am looking for. There's a wardrobe, and two chairs, and a big, old-fashioned chest of drawers which is taller than I am. It has two wide drawers at the bottom, which are very hard to pull open and contain sheets and blankets, and two pairs of smaller drawers above them, which contains socks and underwear. Each of the wide drawers has two wooden knobs on it. Each of the narrower ones has a single wooden knob. And then it has a kind of rectangular decoration above the drawers: a

126

raised rectangle of shiny wood that doesn't seem to serve any purpose. Except that it looks like a drawer with no handles. I hold it as tightly as I can with my fingertips, and pull. It moves. It is a drawer.

The inside of the drawer smells of old lady's perfume. There is some jewelry, an ivory chess set, several packets of rubber johnnies, some yucky-looking stuff in a tube with a broken lid, another two vibrators (one of which is covered in dried yucky stuff) and two nudie magazines. I take out the magazines and look at them on the floor, behind the bed, so that people won't see the torch moving.

The first one is called 'Whitehouse'. It has hardly any pictures in it. It seems to be full of writing, but the writing doesn't look like the writing in Mayfair. Most of it seems to be about something rude, but I haven't time to read it. There are a lot of adverts for films and books and other magazines, and vibrators. One of the adverts has a picture of a woman and an Alsatian dog. When I finally get to some pictures, they're not like the ones in Mayfair. Some of them are in black and white. The women in Mayfair are all in rooms in posh houses, or in the gardens of posh houses or stately homes. They have really nice hair and nice underwear. The women in Whitehouse are in ordinary houses, which aren't even as nice as my house. Some of them look a bit dingy. There are fewer pictures of each woman in Whitehouse than there are in Mayfair. In some of them, the woman is holding her vulva open with her fingers, so you can see up her vagina. The women in Mayfair never do that. In some of the pictures in Whitehouse, you can see the woman's anus, which you can't in Mayfair. I wish they could get the same models in Mayfair to pose like the ones in Whitehouse.

The second magazine is called 'Knave'. I am just about to open it when I hear a noise outside the house that sounds like someone coming in. I quickly put everything back where I found it, close the drawer, and turn the torch off. There is some light coming in from the streetlights at the front of the house. As I am going down the stairs, my eyes adjust to the darkness, and I get all the way down without tripping. I don't think anybody actually came in. No lights have been switched on. I leave the house by the same way I came in. I lock the door behind me and get back on my bike.

When I get home, I can hear them all talking in the sitting room. Everybody is laughing at something. Natalie sounds as if she is in a good mood. I still have Marjorie Rosewall's keys in my coat pocket. I'll

127

put them back during dinner. I hang my coat up in the hall, near the downstairs toilet. I'll ask to get up from the table to go for a wee. Natalie will say, 'Make sure you wash your hands afterwards.' If I actually need a wee, I'll have one, and then I'll wash my hands, in case Natalie checks that my hands smell of soap, and then I'll take the keys out of my coat pocket and slip into the sitting room while everybody is in the dining room. There is a folding partition between the dining room and the sitting room, but Natalie has not opened it this evening.

I wish I had had longer at the Rosewall's. I wanted to see if there were any pictures of Danni in Knave. I am glad there were no pictures of Danni in Whitehouse, even though I would love to see more of her vagina. I don't think Danni should appear in Whitehouse. I think she should only appear in the magazines with the posh houses in the background, and she should concentrate on her degree. I wonder if she'll carry on as a nude model after she starts her career. I wonder if I'll ever get to meet her. I'd say to her, 'Hello. My name's Danni.' And she'd reply, 'My name's Danni, too.' And I'd say, 'I know. I called myself Danni after you.'

1940

Everything is in black and white.

The crew feels uncertain. We started from Wilhelmshaven in U-123, which is a Type IXB German U-boat. We are bound for Norway. It is known that the torpedoes we are carrying are unreliable, and not as good as the torpedoes used by British submarines. We are supposed to help our army to invade Norway, but we don't know how.

I feel uncomfortable and scared in here, because I am the only female person on board, apart from SS Obersturmführer Fleischmann. She is my dream's version of Natalie. She looks and talks like Natalie, and does the sort of things Natalie would do, but she is called Obersturmführer Fleischmann, and she wears a black, SS uniform. The SS are Hitler's bodyguards. Hitler is not on board the U-boat, but Obersturmführer Fleischmann is here as a political commissar, to ensure that we are all imbued with the spirit of National Socialism and that we stand by our personal oath to the Führer. I am not a Nazi. I hate Hitler. I can't remember how I ended up on this U-boat. The men all have beards and they smell. The air inside the vessel smells of mould and dirty toilets and engine oil. Loaves of black bread, hams and salamis hang from the pipework and sway around with the motion of the hull.

The captain is called Kapitän Walther. He is my dream's version of Walt. The Kapitän has a beard as well, but it is a false beard, because Walt is only two years older than me. Leitender Ingenieur Klingemann is my dream's version of John. I know he is on board, but I hardly ever see him, because he spends all his time in the engine room and rarely comes out. All the bunks are double-occupied. Each crew member works his shift and then wakes the man who has been sleeping in the shared bed. Seaman Rosewand is my dream's version of Arthur. Mayfair Danni in my dream is Mayfair Danni, but wearing more old fashioned clothes, and she was photographed in the grounds of a chateau in France rather than a posh house in England. The photographs are in black and white, not just because everything in this dream is in black and white, but because they are actually in black and white. Mayfair Danni's pictures are on the wall, next to my bunk. I share my bunk with Arthur, but we aren't allowed to sleep in it at the same time. Arthur hates Hitler as well, but we can't talk about our opposition to the Nazi party on board the U-boat, because someone would hear us and report us to Obersturmführer Fleischmann.

Seaman Rosewand and I have both been picked for watch duty. Kapitän Walther orders for us to surface, and we put our coats on and climb up to the conning tower. It is night-time. There is some cloud about, but there is a half moon and the sky is mostly clear. I can see thousands of stars. The sea is choppy but not rough. There is a strong breeze blowing in my face. The conning tower is crowded. Seaman Rosewand is standing next to me, looking through his binoculars. Kapitän Walther looks through the UZO (that's a powerful viewing device with two eye-pieces, like a big pair of binoculars, mounted on a metal pillar). There are three other crewmen whose names I don't know. They all have beards. I've got a pair of binoculars as well. It takes me a long time to get the horizon into focus. When I have done that, I find that the view keeps moving around because my hands are shaking. Eventually, I manage to get a good view by bracing my elbows on the rail that runs round the top of the conning tower. After a while, this starts to hurt. I stay in that position until my arms go practically numb. All I can see is the horizon and, beyond it, a few stars and a few clouds.

I've seen something. It is a tiny black rectangle with two or three even smaller rectangles on top of it. It seems to be moving at right angles to our course. It must be a ship, but I can't see what type. I am about to cry out, when I realise that, as soon as the captain gets to hear about it, he'll change course, and give orders for us to try and sink it. I keep quiet. I look at Seaman Rosewand. After a few minutes, he sees the ship as well. He glances at me. I press my lips together. He nods. We put our binoculars back up to our eyes, and pretend we have not seen anything. I hear a shout from one of the bearded men. He has seen it as well, even though he was supposed to be looking at a different part of the horizon. Kapitän Walther turns the UZO around to check the report. He sees the ship, and identifies it as a British destroyer, probably laden with troops bound for Norway.

'Why didn't you report that as a sighting? It was in your segment,' demands Kapitän Walther.

'Sir, it was in my segment,' says Seaman Rosewand.

'No, it wasn't – and, if I want your opinion, I'll ask for it. Until then, please remain silent. Well?'

'I don't know, Herr Kapitän.'

'Falling asleep on the job – that's what you've been doing. Well, I class this as something that needs to be firmly dealt with.' He issues orders to one of the other seamen. 'Take this miscreant down to the brig. Report what has happened to Obersturmführer Fleischmann, and wait below until I arrive. I'll be there in a few minutes. And prepare to dive.'

The brig is a small room with metal bulkheads for walls, a door that can only be opened from the outside, and pipes running along it above head height and near the floor. The pipes are used to tie prisoners to. The captain arrives soon after I am deposited there by the crewman. Through the open door, I can see Seaman Rosewand trying to peer inside from a few metres away.

Kapitän Walther consults with Obersturmführer Fleischmann. While they decide what to do with me, the crew tie my hands and feet to the pipework.

'Death?'

'Definitely death,' says Obersturmführer Fleischmann.

'By what means?'

'Fire her out of a torpedo tube.'

'Mm. Okay.'

'Stripped.'

'What?'

'She'll have to be completely stripped, in case the body is discovered.'

'Yes, of course.'

The crewmen start cutting my clothes off with carving knives, jackknives and penknives. When I am completely naked, they untie me, and lead me to the forward torpedo chamber. I can feel the boat manoeuvring towards the British destroyer. I feel frozen.

In the torpedo chamber, I can see all four of the forward torpedo tubes being loaded. The order comes through to fire Tube One. One of the smelly men starts a stopwatch. After 53 seconds, we all hear a report. The torpedo exploded. Either the detonator was faulty, or it hit its target. After a few more seconds, I can hear cheering from the bridge. That must mean that someone has seen the British destroyer through the periscope, and it has been hit. Many brave men are about to drown in icy water. There is also a vacant torpedo tube.

131

They are preparing a metal cylinder, which is the same diameter as a torpedo, and has the same propulsion mechanism, but no warhead. Obersturmführer Fleischmann arrives in the forward section.

'I want a last request,' I tell her. She does that thing where she heaves her shoulders, turns her face upwards, tilts her head to one side, and rolls her eyes to express annoyance.

'What last request?'

'I want to be escorted to my quarters for a minute.'

'Oh, all right, then.'

Two of the smelly, bearded seamen escort me to my bunk. I am naked. I take Mayfair Danni's pictures off the wall and fold them up as tightly as I can.

'It'll be all right,' I say to Mayfair Danni.

'Don't worry,' I hear a voice in response.

'Why not?'

'Didn't I tell you? I also do mermaid shoots. I can just turn into a mermaid and swim away. I can't do anything for you, but I'll be fine.'

'Don't worry about me.'

'But you are going to drown.'

'Don't worry about me.' I open Danni's centrefold for a second. Where you could see her bum and her legs before, now there is just a big fish tail. I can hear my bare feet padding on the floor of the submarine as I am escorted back to the torpedo chamber.

Seaman Rosewand looks on as they stuff me into the metal cylinder. It feels cramped, but I am much smaller than the inner workings of a torpedo. They try to get me to crawl into it head first and, when that doesn't work, they hold the cylinder at an angle and crewmen feed me into it, feet first. Once inside, I can feel them lift the cylinder and put it into Tube One. I can also feel the submarine descending to a greater depth.

A great heat develops under my feet, from which I recoil. As it moves up the tube, it feels nice, but the soles of my feet are scalded. I hear a rushing noise, and I feel myself being fired out of the submarine into the North Sea. Everything is in black and white.

1981

Walt is having a problem with a *U-Roy* album called *Natty Rebel*. This has been his favourite record for some time now. He is gradually going off *2 Tone* and ska and moving more towards reggae. He has started referring to things like *The Police* as "white man's reggae". I have not bothered to point out to him that he is white, and male. The problem with the album is that the disc is bent. Walt claims to know nothing about how this happened. Whatever it was must have applied considerable force. There is a clearly-visible line running nearly radially along the vinyl. If you look at the record sideways-on, you can see that the radial groove has bent the record out of true by about 5 millimetres. When Walt tries to play it, the arm of the record player jumps like nobody's business. He tries sticking coins onto the head of the arm with little bits of Blu Tack, but that makes no difference. John comes into the playroom to find out what all the weird noises are, and tells Walt off when he sees what he is doing to the record arm. The record player in the playroom was built by John. He never uses it, but he expects everybody else to treat it as if it were his.

Walt goes off in a sulk, which he claims is so that he can think of what to do next. When he returns, I tell him to go into town and buy another copy, but he is convinced he can fix it. His hypothesis is that the application of mild heating will enable the record to revert to its original shape. He puts the record in the microwave oven for a minute. Nothing happens. He puts it in for another minute. Nothing happens. I try to point out to him that the thing that microwave ovens heat, apart from metallic conductors, which you should never put inside them, is water, but the record doesn't contain water. He won't listen. Now he is putting the record onto a baking tray, and turning the gas oven to gas mark a half. He only wants to heat it gently. He waits next to the cooker. Natalie is doing something upstairs, otherwise she would go mad with him. He opens the door of the oven after two minutes. No change. He opens it again after five minutes. No change. Ten minutes. No change. He turns the oven up a little bit, to gas mark 2. He goes away for another ten minutes and comes back to find that the record has completely liquefied. Now he has the problem of explaining to Natalie how he came to destroy a fairly new baking tray. This is not going to be made any easier by the fact that Natalie will probably realise that he will want to replace the record, but he has been banned from spending any of his pocket money on records until further notice. At least none of it went inside the oven, and it hasn't caught fire.

While Walt is gibbering over his molten vinyl, Arthur comes to call for him.

'You have not forgotten we are going in to town, have you?' says Arthur.

'What are you going in to town for?' I ask.

'We are going to buy some chemicals,' replies Arthur.

'What sort of chemicals?'

'None of your business,' says Walt. This is a harsh thing to say, because Walt knows that I would never tell Natalie or John about any of this without checking with him first.

'Flammable chemicals. We are going to have a go at making fireworks,' says Arthur. He takes a piece of paper out of his coat pocket. It contains a list of the substances that he and Walt are intending to buy. Natalie comes in. Arthur looks as if he wants to stuff the list back into his pocket, but knows that that would look suspicious. I am disappointed in Arthur that he writes things down on little bits of paper, rather than using a proper notebook, like I do. Bits of paper always get lost.

'Where are you two going?' asks Natalie.

'Into town,' says Walt.

'You're not thinking of buying any records, are you?'

'Nah,' says Walt.

'What are you going to buy, then?'

'Chemicals,' says Walt.

'Oh,' says Natalie, looking surprised. She leaves the kitchen for a minute, and comes back with some money. She gives Walt a ten pound note. 'None of that is to be spent on records. It is for buying chemicals only. Is that clear?'

'Yeah,' says Walt. He likes to say "nah" and "yeah" because he knows it annoys Natalie. Arthur looks puzzled. I am guessing that he has not told his parents about any of this. Natalie has not noticed the vinyl-covered baking tray yet. Walt and Arthur are just about to leave to catch the bus, and so I will be the first person who will have to deal with the situation when Natalie starts doing her nut about the baking tray. There will be nothing for it but to tell her the truth. Walt will resent me, and probably accuse me of having dropped him in it, but it is his own fault for having done such a stupid thing. Walt seems to have no instinctive grasp of how to interact with the physical universe.

Natalie looks at Walt, and at Arthur, and she looks as if she is about to say something.

'Can Sarah go with you?' It sets my teeth on edge every time she utters the word "Sarah". Walt does not say anything. He just looks back at Natalie. Arthur looks from Walt to Natalie. He looks at me, and smiles a little bit. Walt has his leather purse in his hands and starts tossing it repeatedly into the air, spinning it, and watching it as it rises and falls. This is his way of telling Natalie that he wants to end the conversation and leave the house. 'When you come back, can Sarah at least observe the experiments?' Arthur looks at me. He is still smiling. I don't want him to walk out of the kitchen door and get the bus to town. I want him to stay here, with me. In the hall, a door slams.

'WHAT EXPERIMENTS?' shouts John, through the door between the kitchen and the hall.

'We are going to make some fireworks,' says Walt, still spinning his purse in the air.

'STOP! DON'T LEAVE THIS HOUSE UNTIL I SAY SO.'

I tiptoe into the hall to see what John is doing. He is rooting around in the drawers of his writing desk in the sitting room. He finds something flat and brown. It is an old exercise book, quarto, wide feint and margin. On the cover it says, 'John Richards 3.1A', underlined. He flicks through it. It has writing in it, in faded ink, probably Parker Royal Blue Washable. Some of the pages are stained with brown splotches, some of which have eaten little holes in the paper. John goes into the kitchen, and gives the exercise book to Walt, who stops juggling with his purse. Walt and Arthur put the exercise book between them on the kitchen table, and glance through it. Arthur takes out the list of chemicals and a pen, and adds a few items to it, but I can't see what he is writing. I don't want to hang around in the kitchen for much longer, because I don't know what John and Natalie are going to do next and, if Natalie is left on her own, she will probably try to drag me into something that I don't want to do. John starts going on about the best places to get potassium nitrate and I go back into the hall, and climb the stairs as quietly as I can.

135

I have rearranged my wardrobe so that all the short clothes are hanging at one end, and all the long clothes, of which I do not have many, are at the other. I have also moved the boxes that were under my bed into the bottom of the chest of drawers, which was empty, and my shoes from the wardrobe to under the bed. This means that I can put two pillows on the floor of the wardrobe and lie on them, without clothes dangling in my face. I can also plug my desk-lamp in, and put it on the floor next to me, so that I can see to work. I have checked this arrangement from outside and it is quite easy to position the lamp so that Natalie can't see it through the cracks around the wardrobe doors if she opens my bedroom door and looks in. I might save up for another desk-lamp, the same as the one I've got, and have one on the desk and one inside the wardrobe, so I won't have to keep moving it all the time.

Sometimes, when I'm not working, I move the pillow slightly out of the way and lie on my front, with my face very close to the carpet. I pretend that there is a microphone and a speaker embedded in the carpet, and a wire going under the carpet from where I am to where Mayfair is in Walt's room, and that Mayfair Danni can hear me, and speak to me. We are both people who live in wardrobes, except that we don't really live in wardrobes. We hide in wardrobes, and go inside when we want to be alone.

Sometimes I talk to the other models, but none of them are as interesting to talk to as Mayfair Danni. I don't think Mayfair Danni minds.

I keep all my notebooks and drawings in here. It is a bit cramped for accurate drawing, but OK for thinking and working things out in rough. I used to use squared paper, but now I've got two drawing boards and a small T-square. I am working on another plan. This is nothing to do with the plan of the house I drew I drew three years ago. I am drawing a plan of the place where Mayfair Danni and I want to live. It is in Iceland, and it looks like a castle. It has a moat and a drawbridge and a portcullis. The walls are made of stone. I drew the walls on my larger drawing board, and now I'm drawing the detail of the interior. Instead of a keep, there is a house inside the walls, with two floors, and a helipad on the roof. I have drawn a plan of each floor, and now I am drawing detailed plans of each room. Mayfair Danni and I each have our own bedroom, both the same size. I am drawing my bedroom at the moment. It has a bed which is 2.2 metres wide and 2.0 metres long. On one side is a set of drawers and bookshelves. On the other is a Sony music centre with a turntable, amplifier, double cassette deck, and tuner. I don't know if you can get Radio 4 long wave in Iceland, but you should be able to get the World Service. Next to the music centre is a control panel for the lights, the curtains, and the heating. There is a secret compartment in one of the drawers next to the bed, which contains a radio transmitter, a Commando knife, a 9mm automatic pistol with three spare magazines, and a first aid kit. The bedroom has a sink with a draining board in it, as well as an en suite bathroom. Next to the draining board is a worktop with a kettle and a toaster, and a fridge, so I can make tea and coffee and hot chocolate without having to go downstairs.

It is a while since the automatic pistol was cleaned, and so I had better do that before I do anything else. And then I need to have another talk with Mayfair Danni about what layout she wants in her room. I suppose she'll need more wardrobe space than I do, and she'll probably want a big dressing table.

I think I'm falling asleep. Just before I doze off completely, I move onto my side, and take the cork board I have been resting the paper on, and move it between the pillow and my head, with the raised edge of the board just under my ear. That means that I feel all the time as if I am just about to go to sleep, but I don't actually do it. This is the best way to talk to Mayfair Danni. I'm asking her questions about how much space she wants between the edge of her bed and the wall, and I'm pretending to write down measurements, but I'm not really listening to what she's saying. I like listening to her voice, but I'm just hearing the sound of the words rather than the meaning. She's wearing the same outfit she wears on page 89, which is the last page she appears on. I'm lying on my side on the bed in my room, and she is kneeling on the floor a few feet away, facing half away from me. I can see her bare bum, and the curve of her back, and the soles of her shoes. She glances at me half over her shoulder as she talks. Every so often, she pouts her lips at me, especially when she's asking me for more space, or something more difficult or expensive to fit. I tell her that it is only fair if our rooms are both the same size, and she starts blinking at me, and she pouts more, and she shakes her long, curly, blonde hair. She turns round to face me. Her breasts are bare. It is so long since she took her bra off, you can't even see any marks on her skin where the straps were. She starts stroking her nipples. She looks down at them, and then back at me, and she carries on stroking them while she is talking. I tell her that she can arrange things inside the room any way she wants, but the size of the room can't be increased. She opens her mouth, rests the tip of her tongue behind her top teeth, and starts pinching her nipples. She pinches them again, harder, both of them at the same time. She pinches them again, even harder. She gasps.

That's Arthur and Walt coming back. I don't want them to come back at this moment. I want to stay with Mayfair Danni.

I'm still trying to wake up fully as I go downstairs to see what they have bought. The worst time for Natalie to come looking for me is when I am with Mayfair Danni. A minute ago I felt warm. Now I feel too hot, and prickly, and I've got a headache. Headaches are not allowed in this house.

When I arrive in the kitchen, Natalie and John are talking to Walt and Arthur.

'I think you should let Sarah join in,' says Natalie.

'Nah,' says Walt.

'Why not?' says John.

'She's a girl,' says Walt. Arthur is looking from one person to another. He keeps putting his hands in his trouser pockets, and quickly taking them out again. 'She's too young,' says Walt. Nobody says anything. 'Arthur and I want to do it on our own.' John and Arthur look at each other.

'Do you mind if Sarah joins in?' John asks Arthur.

'No, I don't mind at all,' Arthur replies. My headache starts to feel better. Arthur takes his spectacles off and tries to clean them on his handkerchief. He realises the handkerchief is dirty, and then pulls his shirt out of his waistband and tries to clean them on the hem of the shirt.

'She doesn't know anything about chemicals,' says Walt.

'Sarah,' says John, turning to me, 'Which is the stronger oxidising agent: potassium permanganate, or hydrogen peroxide?'

'Potassium permanganate. A strong, acidic solution will oxidise most organic compounds to carbon dioxide and water.'

'What reagent would I use to react with iodine to make a colourless solution?'

'Sodium thiosulphate.'

'What is the ratio of sulphur to oxygen atoms in the molecular formula of sodium thiosulphate?'

'Two to three.' John puts his hands behind his back, looks at Arthur, raises his eyebrows, and then looks at Walt. Walt looks down.

I start to explain the rudiments of the periodic table to Mayfair Danni in my head while everybody else has a conversation about eye protection. I don't think she gets it. Arthur does not need any additional eye protection, because he wears spectacles, and I do not need any because I will not be getting near enough to the site of any reaction to be in any danger. John goes into his workshop, and comes back with a pair of safety goggles for Walt, a bag of barbecue charcoal, and a wooden pestle and mortar that I remember used to be in the kitchen a few years ago, before Natalie got a granite one as a replacement.

'Why don't you get Sarah to grind the charcoal?' asks John.

Arthur picks up two carrier bags full of jars, boxes, and bottles. We go outside.

Sarah grinds the charcoal. While Sarah grinds the charcoal, Walt and Arthur try to make gunpowder out of potassium nitrate, flowers of sulphur, and charcoal which has been ground by placing a piece of lumpwood charcoal on the paved area at the bottom of the back garden and then stamping on it with Walt's desert boot. Walt has an outside chance of covering this paved area in black stuff, and neglecting to sweep it up, without getting done. As I am working, I keep looking up at the thing in which we used to play the aeroplane-spaceship-submarine games. It is rotting. The wooden frame, the sheets of Perspex, and the bits of electrical appliances are not sheltered from the weather.

Walt's gunpowder is pathetic. It reminds me of those bits in 'Blue Peter' when they say they are going to show you how to make something but they don't really go through with it, because they have got the schedule wrong and they don't have enough time. It doesn't burn uniformly. It sputters, because the charcoal isn't sufficiently finely-divided. While Walt tries stamping harder and harder, I grind away with the pestle and mortar. The trick is to do it one piece at a time, and never allow the mortar to get full of big bits. You have to press really hard, and twist the pestle both ways. There is a magic moment when it goes from being hundreds or thousands of little crunchy bits, to innumerable, velvety, microscopic particles.

When I have ground enough charcoal to keep the boys entertained for the afternoon, I dip the end of my little finger in it, and taste it. No grittiness. Smooth. You could stir a spoonful of that into someone's coffee and they wouldn't notice until the very end.

Walt and Arthur are having a little rest. They talk about reggae music. Walt tries to talk to Arthur about model trains, but Arthur only pretends to be interested.

I go into the house for a minute to get some things. When I get back, I take a thick pencil. One of the ones that were bought from E. J. Arnold but which I never use. I take a piece of card from the backing of a pad I used up a long time ago. I take a pair of scissors and cut the card. I roll the card around the pencil. I fasten the cardboard tube with parcel tape. I block the bottom of the tube with a piece torn off a tampon.

I dump the contents of the mortar into an empty carrier bag from the boys' shopping trip. I measure out 75 parts potassium nitrate, 15 parts of my finely-divided charcoal, and 10 parts flowers of sulphur. I mix them together thoroughly in the mortar with a spoon. I pour the powder onto a paper and then pour it into the cardboard tube. Every so often, I tamp it down with the thick pencil. I keep going until the tube is full.

I give it to the boys. They've got the matches. I put some stones on the paved area, and place the firework among the stones. It is reasonably stable and reasonably vertical.

They light a match. It goes out. They light another match. It goes out. They light another match. They cup their hands around it, and it goes out.

I grab the matchbox from their hands. I am lying on the ground. I take three matches out of the box, and cast away the un-struck ones. I make sure that I have got three live ones. I strike them, and put them to the mouth of the firework propped among the stones.

Whoooooooooosh! It burns evenly, with an intense whitish-yellow flame and only a little smoke, which smells of sulphur. It burns faster and faster as the flame front descends into the tube and the effusing gas increases in pressure. BANG! A little explosion at the end. The small pile of stones is demolished, revealing the cardboard tube with the torn-off tampon blown out and the cardboard splayed in all directions.

The boys thought that was amazing. I'm going back to the wardrobe. I want to have another try at explaining the periodic table to Mayfair Danni.

1982

Arthur and Walt have read a page in John's exercise book which describes an explosive called nitrogen tri-iodide. You make it by mixing iodine with ammonia solution and then allowing the resulting solid to dry out. The pages which describe this reaction are the most stained in the whole book. The stains are mostly a purplish-brown colour, like the bruise around Walt's left eye.

I have come across this substance before, in a textbook, which said, "this is a mere chemical curiosity: it is too unstable to be considered a practical explosive".

Arthur and Walt came back from a trip to the chemist shops in town with a small, glass bottle containing two grams of iodine, for which they paid two pounds and thirty-eight pence. John laughed, and came back from work the following day with a brown jar which looked about seventy years old. Inside was about half a kilogram, and it cost nothing. They already had a bottle of ammonia solution which they got from a stall in the market which sells cleaning stuff. The instructions say that the best method is to place a small piece of solid iodine at the centre of a circle of filter paper, fold the paper into quarters, and then dip the portion containing the iodine into the ammonia solution. As soon as the paper is thoroughly dry, the nitrogen tri-iodide is ready to detonate. As John wrote in his book, "the touch of a fly's wing is enough to set it off".

I can see them through the playroom window. Walt pours a ridiculous amount of ammonia solution into a plastic ice-cream container. He and Arthur can't help inhaling ammonia and they start wheezing and coughing, theatrically at first and then for real. They have to keep moving away from the plastic container to gulp lungsful of uncontaminated air. They have a plentiful supply of filter paper and of the iodine from the big, brown jar. They have no eye protection, except for Arthur's spectacles, which have glass lenses which might shatter, and no gloves. They are talking as they work. I can't hear them, but I can tell that they are not talking about what they are doing, or even anything to do with chemistry.

It starts to rain. They look up at the sky and decide that they need to come inside. They saunter back up the garden, still carrying the ice-cream tub full of aqueous ammonia and the damp filter papers containing the nitrogen tri-iodide. Natalie is cooking in the kitchen, and goes mad with them. The stench of ammonia starts to mingle with the smell of frying onions and rosemary and white sauce in Natalie's pans. Somehow, that seems even worse than the smell of ammonia on its own. She sends them outside, back the way they came.

'Where are we supposed to put all this stuff?' asks Walt.

'I don't care, as long as you get it out of here immediately!' That leaves them with only two options: John's workshop or the shed. Even Walt realises that putting anything that does not belong to John in John's workshop is asking for trouble. They reluctantly pour the ammonia solution down the drain, put the filter papers into the empty tub, and leave the tub in the shed. They come inside and, before they wash their hands, they leave traces of nitrogen tri-iodide on every doorknob and surface they touch. You can tell where they have been by the strange noises caused by the reaction. It is an unexpected "shush" noise, which makes you wonder if you have just heard a tiny explosion, but is over too quickly for you to be sure what it is. Sometimes, the site of the explosion is marked by a little purplish-brown smudge. Walt and Arthur go upstairs to Walt's bedroom to play with the model railway and listen to reggae. Walt and Arthur's school year has its annual disco tonight. My year's is next week. I am going to be wearing a suit like the one Pauline Black from The Selecter wears.

The next day is Sunday. John goes out early to mow the lawn in the back garden. He goes into the shed to get some weed-killer. He nudges the plastic tub containing the nitrogen tri-iodide, which has had time to dry out. It explodes. I hear it from my bedroom. I rush downstairs in my pyjamas. John has staggered back to the kitchen door. His face is white. His hands are shaking. Natalie asks him if he is all right, over and over again, but it seems that he can't hear properly. Natalie gets John to sit on a chair in the kitchen while she makes him a cup of tea with two sugars. While Natalie is making the tea, John gets up and goes upstairs. I follow him. John goes into Walt's bedroom. Walt is still asleep. I put my head round the door. I don't think John knows I am there.

John grabs Walt by the material of the top he is wearing and starts to drag him out of bed.

'IF YOU EVER DO ANYTHING LIKE THAT AGAIN, I WILL COME DOWN ON YOU LIKE A TON OF BRICKS!' he shouts. Walt's eyes are open, but he has no idea what John is talking about. He must have slept through the explosion. Walt is half out of bed, with one foot on the floor and his head resting awkwardly on the bed-frame. John pulls him up and drops him again, again and again. Walt has nothing to brace his left arm against, and so can't stop himself from dropping each time John lets go of him. His head bangs against the edge of the wooden bed-frame.

I go into my room and lie inside the wardrobe. I can hear John shouting at Walt, and Walt shouting at John. I can hear more banging, and things being knocked over. John stomps downstairs. I just hear silence for a few minutes, and then I can faintly hear the sound of a train going round the model railway. A bit later, I hear *Concrete Jungle* by Bob Marley and the Wailers. As soon as the song finishes, he plays it again. He has started a habit of playing the same track over and over again, and recording it on both sides of a cassette, so he can listen to it ad nauseam without having to fiddle about with the record player. When he has made a tape with the same song filling up both sides, he listens to it on his Walkman while he goes for one of his long walks. I expect Walt will go for a long walk after this.

Walt's music stops after a while. I can hear him moving around, but I can't work out what he is doing. I start to feel hungry after a while, and so I get dressed and go downstairs. Walt is already there. He is putting his coat and shoes on, and there is a cup of tea on the kitchen table which he is in the middle of drinking. Natalie is moving things around in the larder. I don't know where John is. Walt picks up a satchel and starts to put some things into it. John comes in, from outside.

'What are you doing?' asks John.

'Getting ready to go out,' says Walt.

'Where do you think you might be going?'

'Arthur's house.'

'Is this something you have already arranged?'

'Yes. I arranged it with Arthur, yesterday.'

'GET IN THERE.' John points to the hall, where the downstairs phone is. 'Phone Arthur, and apologise to him for the fact that you can't see him. You are going to be doing jobs for me today – I've got plenty of weeding, and painting, and other stuff for you to do.'

Walt leaves the door to the hall open while he is on the phone. Natalie has emerged from the larder, and she, John, and I listen to Walt's side of the conversation.

'Uh. Hello, Mrs Rosewall. This is David Richards. Can I speak to Arthur, please? Arthur? It's Walt. I can't come round. John says I have to do jobs in the garden this afternoon. Sorry. Yes. See you at school tomorrow. Sorry. Yes. No. Bye.' Walt comes back into the kitchen. John looks pleased. Walt takes his satchel off and John escorts him outside into the garden. Natalie goes back into the larder. I start to make myself some toast. I am just deciding whether to eat the toast in the kitchen, or risk taking it upstairs, when the phone rings. Natalie goes to answer it. The hall door is still open. I find that I can get quite close to the door without Natalie seeing me. Mrs Rosewall is talking so loudly that I can hear most of what she is saying.

'Oh, hello Marjorie. How are you?'

'Pretty bloody incensed, as a matter of fact, Natalie.'

'Oh.'

'Arthur tells me that Walt just rang up to say that he couldn't keep to the arrangement that they had made yesterday.'

'Er, yes.'

'I was going to take them to a book and record fair in Ilkley. Arthur is disappointed. They were looking forward to it.'

'Oh.'

'What the hell is going on?'

'David – er – Walt did something for which John feels he needs to be punished, and so he has told him that – '

'No. Sorry. Got to stop you there, Natalie. Punishing Walt is one thing. Punishing my child is quite another. Arthur and I are all ready to go. You get Walt over here, pronto. Whatever you do with him after we come back from Ilkley is up to you, but a deal's a deal. Right?' Natalie doesn't say anything. 'Right?'

'Er. Yes, Marjorie. I'll talk to John. I'll bring Walt round as soon as I can.'

'Not as soon as you can – immediately.'

'Yes.'

'You do know what "immediately" means, don't you?'

'Yes. Yes, of course.'

'This is a kind of conversation I do not want to have with you again.'

'No. No, of course not.'

Natalie goes outside to talk to John and Walt. Walt comes back in with a smile on his face. He picks his satchel up and finishes getting ready. He checks his purse, which seems to have money in it. I go into the playroom. I can see Natalie trying to explain to John what Marjorie said, and John shouting. I can't decide whether or not to go outside to hear what they are saying. I decide not to.

I go upstairs and get into the wardrobe. I am not writing or drawing. I am just lying in the dark, with the door closed and the lamp off. After a few minutes, I can hear John coming upstairs. He is shouting for Sarah. He opens the door of my bedroom; shuts it again. He goes into Walt's room. He goes into the upstairs bathroom, his and Natalie's bedroom, the guest bedroom, his study. He keeps shouting for Sarah. He does another inspection of the upstairs rooms, this time opening all the wardrobes and cupboards. I can hear his stomping footsteps. I can hear him slamming doors and swearing, and shouting for Sarah.

I have to get out of the wardrobe. I don't want him to know that I live in the wardrobe. If he finds out where I live, he will do something to it: nail it shut, or fill it with boxes, or start searching it. When he opens the door of my room a second time, I am sitting on my bed, not doing anything.

'Where did you spring from?'

'Nowhere.'

I really don't feel like gardening. I wonder if Walt and Arthur are having a nice time in Ilkley.

1941

Everything is in black and white.

I am lying in my bunk. I feel very tired, but I am awake, looking at some new pictures of Mayfair Danni I got for this voyage. I know I only have a few minutes before the crewman I share this bunk with will arrive and will want to get into it immediately. This crewman isn't Arthur: it is someone else: someone I don't know and don't talk to. If I am not out of the bunk and standing up by the time he arrives at the end of his shift, he just lies down on top of me. He is heavy and he smells.

Mayfair Danni looks beautiful in the new pictures. She is in the grounds of another French chateau. It has high towers with conical rooves which make it look like something out of a fairytale. It looks like a place we visited once when we were on holiday in the Loire valley, when I was about five. Mayfair Danni is wearing a milkmaid's outfit. In some of the pictures, she is carrying a wooden yoke with buckets hanging from it. The outfit has a long black skirt with a white pinafore, and a red, lace-up bodice with white lace round the edge, and white, blouson sleeves. The red bodice shows red in the dream. In the fourth picture in the sequence, she unlaces it to expose her breasts. If I put my face right up to the picture, I can talk to her, and I don't have to raise my voice above a whisper.

I have to get up now.

Morale among the crew is high. The problem with the reliability of the torpedoes has been fixed. We have fired seven so far on this mission, and none has been a dud.

Walt is no longer the captain. In this dream, he has been demoted to section leader of the torpedo operators. I am part of that section. Arthur is not on board. Natalie is still Obersturmführer Fleischmann. The captain is now John. He is called Kapitän Klingemann.

It is night. We are in the North Atlantic, submerged, and Kapitän Klingemann is looking at a passenger liner through the periscope. It is called the *SS Europa*. It is travelling along a course at right-angles to ours, and is about 1400 metres away, at a bearing of about 340 degrees: slightly to our left, in other words, and heading towards our right. It is doing 20 knots, which is miles faster than us, and faster even than we could manage if we were on the surface. If the captain decides to attack the liner, we will only have one chance to sink it or to cripple it enough so that it has to slow down to our speed. The captain orders us to prepare for a submerged attack. The four forward tubes are already loaded. Walt and I and the other torpedo crew are moving some torpedoes forward, to put them into the positions vacated by the ones that have been loaded into the tubes. I watch Walt attaching an iron hook on the end of a chain to the torpedo. The hook is one of a set of four. The chains are wound onto pulleys above our heads, which move on rails. Walt is talking to one of the other crew, and not looking at what he is doing.

When he pulls on the chains to raise the torpedo off the rack, it gets about two feet up, and then the two hooks at the front work loose. The front of the torpedo, the end with the warhead in it, falls and crashes to the floor, missing my right food by six inches. A metallic clang reverberates through every steel plate in the hull, and through every man's bones. The members of the torpedo section dart glances at each other, and at the half-suspended torpedo, as if wondering whether it is going to detonate. We hear footsteps approaching at a quick pace, and the hatch opening.

'WHAT THE HELL WAS THAT?' No-one bothers to answer, as Kapitän Klingemann glowers at the torpedo. He flicks a chain, one of the ones that worked loose. 'Who was responsible for failing to secure these? How many times have I told you to double-check all hooks before taking the strain? How many times have I told you that you endanger the whole vessel and the life of every man on it by your carelessness?' No-one speaks. 'Get this weapon back on the rack. Don't mess about with anything else until I give the order. In the meantime, we are just about to attack. Fire tubes one and two. I will finish dealing with this incident after we have completed our action against the enemy vessel.'

We are ideally positioned to fire at the *Europa*. It takes two hits almost simultaneously, and starts to sink. We surface. I can't see what is happening for a while, because I have to stay below, and am not ordered up to the conning tower.

After a while, I can hear some activity from the conning tower. We seem to be bringing some of the survivors aboard, though it can only be a handful of them out of the hundreds or even thousands who must have been on the liner. I timidly go through the hatch, towards the bridge. I can see a small group of survivors. I can see that, under the damp, grey blankets they are wrapped in, they are wearing evening dress. I recognise three of them. They are Mr and Mrs Rosewall and Arthur. Arthur is called Rosewall in this dream and not Rosewand, because he is on the Allied side. I am too far away for them to see me, but I can hear what they are saying.

'This is monstrous. Your action is in clear violation of international law,' says Mrs Rosewall.

'Marjorie, I am sorry you feel that way, but you are wrong. Since a state of war exists between our two nations, I am entitled to fire on an enemy vessel,' says Kapitän Klingemann.

'Not when it is an unarmed civilian vessel, you are not.'

'Your ship was clearly armed. We could see that guns had been mounted. You British will insist on doing this, in clear breach of international treaties. Take them away and put them in the brig. Now, I must attend to the situation in the forward torpedo room.'

I run back to where I came from.

Kapitän Klingemann stands in front of Walt.

'Who was responsible for the torpedo working loose from the pulley?' Walt does not say anything. None of the other crewmen say anything. Walt just stands to attention and looks into space. He still has bruises round one eye, but in the dream they are grey instead of brown and purple.

'It was me,' someone says. Kapitän Klingemann looks round. He did not notice who said it. I said it. 'It was me, sir.' I say it again. Kapitän Klingemann looks sideways at me. Walt is still standing to attention.

'A member of your section appears to have let you off the hook, Seaman Walther, just like the front end of the torpedo.' He turns to me. I stand to attention. 'In view of the potentially catastrophic nature of this accident, and the fact that you have admitted it was your fault, I have no choice but to make an example of you to the other members of the crew. Slackness of this kind will not be tolerated on this vessel...' I stop listening to the lecture Kapitän Klingemann is giving me. I just say, 'No, sir,' and 'Yes, sir,' at the right moments. I notice someone come in to the torpedo room. This person is dressed in a black SS uniform and wears an armband with a Nazi swastika. The swastika is black. The circle around the swastika is white, and the rest of the armband is red. It appears red in the dream. It is

149

Obersturmführer Fleischmann. She talks to the captain about what they are going to do with me. I am not listening. After a while, I notice them both nodding, and Kapitän Klingemann giving orders to the crew. One of the crewmen looks about to say something to me. I start taking my uniform off. The crewman has not uttered any words yet, but I know that whatever Obersturmführer Fleischmann and Kapitän Klingemann decided, they are going to have me executed and they will insist that I am naked before I go to my death. The inside of the U-boat, as always, is freezing cold. Every surface is made of metal, and feels like it is coated with ice. The air swirling around my naked body feels nearly as cold as the ship itself, but neither of them are as cold as the sea.

I climb the ladder of the conning tower and down the other side, onto the deck. The hull of the SS Europa is a few hundred metres away and has listed over almost at right-angles, and will have sunk in another minute or two. There are a few lifeboats still in the water, which the crew are finishing off with the deck gun and two machine guns, with the aid of a searchlight. Kapitän Klingemann has had the prisoners brought on deck, still in their damp, grey blankets and shivering almost as much as I am. I can't keep still even if I want to.

Mrs Rosewall is trying to argue with the captain.

'What are you doing to that little girl?' she keeps asking.

'She is being punished,' says the captain.

'What for?'

'Failure to do her duty, and endangering this vessel.' Mrs Rosewall looks as me. The deck of the U-boat pitches. A wave throws spray over us, wetting Mrs Rosewall's evening dress and making me shiver even more.

'Danni! You can come and live with us!' She reaches out to me, but is held back by members of the crew. Someone hits her across the face with the butt of a pistol.

The captain sends an order to the navigator to report to him the depth of the water. We aren't very far off the west coast of Ireland, and so the depth is only 92 metres. The captain orders them to fetch a chain, and cut it to exactly 91.7 metres. They fasten one end of the chain around my neck, and the other end to an iron weight like the ones they use for anchoring sea-mines. I can hear the captain talking about me.

'I want her to be able to see the surface of the water while she's dying, but not be able to breathe.'

'Yes, Herr Kapitän.'

They cast the iron weight into the sea. The chain uncoils quickly as the weight descends. I am pulled into the engulfing cold. The shock nearly stops my heart. I flail around in the water upside down, which makes me panic even more, and then I just relax, and float upright. They got the calculation of the chain length just right. I am floating with my face about six inches below the surface. I can still see the moon, and some of the brighter stars, but I can only inhale water. As I die, I think about what it would be like if Mayfair Danni and I moved to the Rosewall's house. I could play board games with Arthur, and help Mrs Rosewall with the housework, and Mr Rosewall in the garden. Arthur and I could do our homework together after school.

When I wake up, I realise it is a school day, and I have wet the bed.

1984

Apart from the shabby-looking piece of painted hardboard over one of the window-panes, Walt's room is the tidiest I have seen it for a long time, now that the model railway has been torn out. All the mess that Walt left behind on the day he destroyed it has been cleared away by Natalie and me. The only sign that the railway was there are the rows of screw holes along the walls, which we have not had time to fill yet, and the difference in colour of the wallpaper above and below where the plywood base used to be. The room seems much bigger without it. I miss being able to sit underneath the base board. It was a handy place from which to keep an eye on Walt and listen to his music, not all of which was crap, and be out of sight of John and Natalie.

I have kept some of the plastic figures, and put them in an empty box that used to contain filter paper. Walt finished painting a few of the figures. Some of them he started painting but never finished, and some of them are just bare, pale yellow plastic. Walt had a little diorama near the main platform in his station which was a man on a bicycle, being chased by a shaggy, black dog, and a member of the station staff in a dark blue uniform, who Walt always said was telling the man off for cycling within the station concourse. I didn't keep the man in the blue uniform. The transformers, the wiring, the parts of the track that had not been bent or broken, and the rolling stock, John and Natalie have put in a box and are intending to sell by putting an advert in the Leeds Weekly News. As John pointed out, it doesn't cost anything to put an advert in the "For Sale" column of the Leeds Weekly News.

Walt left yesterday. He came in from school, went up to his bedroom, and started pulling out the wooden supports that the model railway rested on, with his bare hands. I tried to talk to him, but he would not listen to me. Natalie came upstairs to find out what the noise was, by which time Walt had the base board off the wall and was trying to break it in half. Natalie went into her and John's bedroom, and just sat on the bed. I was on the upstairs landing, trying to watch both of them at once. I was worried that Walt might hurt himself. If I had wanted to do something like that, I would have got some tools first. He threw one of the wooden supports at the window, like a javelin, and it went straight through. The pane of glass didn't shatter completely: the piece of wood splintered a circular hole about five inches across, with jagged cracks radiating out of it, and points sticking inwards like lamprey teeth. The wood landed on the patio and smashed a pot of marjoram. After Walt had left the house, John came home. He used one of the pieces of the broken base board to cover the hole in the window. It has grass borders, and pavement, and road painted on it, and a bare patch where one of the station platforms used to be. Today is Saturday. John went out a while ago to buy a sheet of glass and some putty. Natalie has gone out with the rambling club.

John and Natalie have been thinking for some time of installing double-glazing. This may be the time when they decide to do it.

I am writing John and Natalie a note. I am leaving. I am going to London to see if Walt is there. I have arranged to stay at a squat in Brixton with a Swedish woman called Gunilla, who I met recently at an anarchist conference in Todmorden. She only knows me as Danni. None of my anarchist friends know I used to be called Sarah. I wanted to pass my exams and go to university, and do a postgraduate degree, like Mayfair Danni, but I can't live here without Walt. I have also posted a letter to Arthur, telling him not to worry about me, and that I was in love with him for a bit and would have let him kiss me if he had wanted to.

I found eighty pounds in one of the drawers of John's writing desk, and I'm taking that with me, but I'm not buying a train ticket. I'll get the bus into Leeds, walk to the start of the M1 and then hitch-hike. There is going to be a big demonstration tomorrow. Gunilla and I will be going on it with the South London Anarchist Group. I wonder if we'll get arrested.

Other novels, novellas and short story collections available from Stairwell Books

The Exhibitionists	Ed. Rose Drew and Alan Gillott
The Green Man Awakes	Ed. Rose Drew
Fosdyke and Me and Other Poems	John Gilham
Along the Iron Veins	Ed. Alan Gillott and Rose Drew
Gringo on the Chickenbus	Tim Ellis
Running With Butterflies	John Walford
Late Flowering	Michael Hildred
Pressed by Unseen Feet	Ed. Rose Drew and Alan Gillott
York in Poetry Artwork and Photographs	Ed. John Coopey and Sally Guthrie
Taking the Long Way Home	Steve Nash
Skydive	Andrew Brown
Still Life With Wine and Cheese	Ed. Rose Drew and Alan Gillott
Somewhere Else	Don Walls
Sometimes I Fly	Tim Goldthorpe
49	Paul Lingaard
Homeless	Ed. Ross Raisin
The Ordinariness of Parrots	Amina Alyal
New Crops from Old Fields	Ed. Oz Hardwick
Throwing Mother in the Skip	William Thirsk-Gaskill
The Problem With Beauty	Tanya Nightingale
Learning to Breathe	John Gilham
Unsettled Accounts	Tony Lucas
Lodestone	Hannah Stone
A Multitude of Things	David Clegg
The Beggars of York	Don Walls
Rhinoceros	Daniel Richardson
More Exhibitionism	Ed. Glen Taylor
Heading for the Hills	Gillian Byrom-Smith
Nothing Is Meant to be Broken	Mark Connors
Northern Lights	Harry Gallagher
The Battle Fiends	E. H. Visiak
Poetry for the Newly Single 40 Something	Maria Stephenson
Gooseberries	Val Horner
A Thing of Beauty Is a Joy Forever	Don Walls
The River Was a God	David Lee Morgan
The Glass King	Gary Allen

For further information please contact rose@stairwellbooks.com
www.stairwellbooks.co.uk
@stairwellbooks